A DRE

Rod caught my arm before I could open the car door. "What's your hurry? Are you going to flit away like one of your famous butterflies?"

"They aren't *my* butterflies. Butterflies are free."

"Speaking of free," he said. "Are you free next Friday?"

With my heart hammering up in my throat, I managed to pretend a calm I didn't feel. "I thought I'd go to the game."

"Yeah, me too," he said with a twinkle in his blue eyes. "I meant later. I thought maybe you'd like to go to the sock hop with me . . ."

Only in Sunshine

Ann Gabhart

AN AVON FLARE BOOK

ONLY IN SUNSHINE is an original publication of Avon Books. This work has never before appeared in book form.

AVON BOOKS
A division of
The Hearst Corporation
105 Madison Avenue
New York, New York 10016

Copyright © 1988 by Ann Gabhart
Published by arrangement with the author
Library of Congress Catalog Card Number: 87-91457
ISBN: 0-380-75395-2
RL: 5.9

First Avon Flare Printing: May 1988

AVON FLARE TRADEMARK REG. U.S. PAT. OFF. AND IN OTHER COUNTRIES, MARCA REGISTRADA, HECHO EN U.S.A.

Printed in the U.S.A.

K-R 10 9 8 7 6 5 4 3 2

To my children—
Johnny, Daniel, and especially Tarasa,
who once had to put together an insect collection
for her science class

Chapter 1

I never planned to be a champion of butterflies. The only thing I was planning to champion when the school year began was myself, because this had to be my year. I was a junior and time was running out.

To prove the signs were right for me, I made a list. First, Jason, my brother, had been off to college for three years and hardly anybody anymore—except for a few teachers—asked if I was his sister while that sneaky, surprised look crept into their eyes. Second, though she would soon, Maddie, my little sister, hadn't started grabbing the headlines quite yet..

There was more on my list about being almost sixteen and having spent the summer not just reading but studying every romance book the library had. I needed lots of reasons because I planned to make some pretty big changes in my life-style. I was tired of being ordinary while everyone around me was special.

Still I couldn't change from a nobody to Miss Popularity of Brookfield High just by making lists and dreaming up reasons why it should happen. I needed something to get the ball rolling. That's where the butterflies came in. Just sort of floating down out of heaven to give me a starting place, though I suppose I could say Rod Westmore was the real starting place.

Rod is one of those super guys who has everything. Sort of like Jason, but Jason was my brother and Rod wasn't. That made Rod a lot more special and a definite target for my self-improvement plans. I mean if I was dating a boy like Rod Westmore, I couldn't be too ordinary, could I?

Tracy, my girlfriend, said that Rod was too full of himself, what with being so great-looking and a football hero, to ever be interested in us and that it might be more sensible to set our sights on one of the other guys. But I was out for the best this year. Besides, Tracy was always finding something wrong with the guys who didn't notice us. It kept her pretty busy since that included nearly the whole male population of Brookfield High.

"He's just shy," I told her last summer as I studied his picture in the annual and remembered how blue his eyes were.

"If he's shy, what's that make us?" Tracy said with a snort. "Petrified?"

"No, really," I insisted. "Lots of good-looking boys are really shy down deep. I read about it the other day in a magazine."

"The writer must not have known Rod Westmore," Tracy said.

Actually I had to admit that Rod didn't act very shy, but he was nice. The first week of classes, when I dropped my pencil in biology class and it rolled up by his foot, he picked it up and handed it back to me with a smile.

Of course he didn't really see me. Not the real Wendi Collins who keeps fighting to get free from

2

this other ordinary girl who's shackled by stoplight-red blushes and brown hair that never knows exactly how it wants to lie on my head. I guess my mouth and nose are all right. I've even been told I have good bones, which is important if you plan to go off to New York and be a model.

But my eyes are hopeless. They don't even know what color they want to be. They wait every morning till I get dressed and then flash green or gray or sometimes with the right light and the right shirt they're almost turquoise blue. I wear that shirt a lot.

I had it on that first day in biology when I discovered Rod and I would be sharing a class—another sign I could add to my list that this would finally be my year.

While Mrs. Lunsford called out our names, I watched Rod out of the corner of my eye as he leaned up against the wall and looked bored with the whole mess and especially Mrs. Lunsford.

Mrs. Lunsford, one of those teachers from the old school who think kids our age don't have enough intelligence to pick our own seats in class, made us stand up by the blackboard while she called out our names alphabetically. Then we trooped over to our seats in proper order. In Mrs. Lunsford's class everything was and stayed in proper order.

She didn't call my name, or at least I don't think she did. Instead I was still standing up by the board after the last person, who just happened to be Rod Westmore, went to his seat.

Mrs. Lunsford looked down at her book and back up at me. "Why aren't you in a seat?"

As my face turned five shades of red, I wanted to sink through the floor, but I summoned up enough nerve to say, "You didn't call my name, Mrs. Lunsford."

"Of course I did." She looked down at her book again. "Wendi Collins. You should be right behind Stewart Campbell."

After a quick glance at Sally Deaton, who occupied the seat in question, Mrs. Lunsford turned her eyes back to me and waited, wordlessly, for an explanation of why Sally was sitting behind Stewie instead of me.

I didn't say anything. I didn't think she'd called out my name, but teachers have a way of not liking to be contradicted. And especially Mrs. Lunsford. Her reputation for absolute authority in her classes carried down even to junior high. "Just wait till you have Scary Mary" was a warning that made the bravest kid tremble. Not brave at all, I was shaking all over as I hugged my notebook a little closer to me and wondered if a person really could die of embarrassment.

After she had stared at me for what seemed like an hour, she motioned me toward the last seat of the last row, the only empty desk. "Tomorrow wash out your ears before you come to class, Miss Collins," she said.

The rest of the class tittered a little, which she allowed for maybe two seconds before she turned on them, and every giggle dried up like water sucked up by a tornado.

I sank down with relief, glad to be out of the spotlight. It was a full minute before I dared look up from my book. My heart beat a little faster as I stared at the back of Rod Westmore's head and decided maybe the embarrassment had been worth the end result.

4

Definitely another sign that this was my year. Then I looked to my left and there was Jeff Sunley.

Jeff is three months older than me to the day and has always lived next door. Our parents are great friends, especially our moms, so Jeff and I shared everything from teethers to chicken pox when we were little. Now it looked like we'd be able to share biology homework, and having Jeff right there across the aisle close enough to whisper to in any other class besides Mrs. Lunsford's made me feel better. By the time the bell rang, my face was almost its normal shade again.

Since it's against the rules to talk on the way out in Mrs. Lunsford's class, I had to wait till we got out in the hall before I could say anything to Jeff. Ahead of us the noise exploded from each group like blasts from a loudspeaker as the kids pushed through the doorway out into the hall.

"Did she call out my name?" I asked Jeff when I stepped through the doorway.

"Nope. Even old Scary Mary makes a mistake from time to time." Jeff grinned, and his green eyes practically danced in his face.

Jeff's nice-looking. Not a Rod Westmore, but still a pretty nice-looking guy. His hair, which used to be just plain red when we were kids, has mellowed to a nice reddish brown. Because he worries about not being very tall, he works out on weights all the time, and it's beginning to show. Looking at him now, I was sort of surprised at the way his new muscles made him look different somehow.

The door slammed shut behind us and made me remember Mrs. Lunsford again. I glanced over my shoulder and said, "I think Mrs. Lunsford thinks I'm the mistake."

"Poor Wendi," Jeff said. "You've never had a teacher who didn't like you before, have you?"

"Oh, I don't know. A lot of my teachers haven't bothered to hide their disappointment when they found out I wasn't as brilliant as Jason."

"You're brilliant enough."

"But not like Jason."

"Not many people are, but you're still always the teacher's pet."

"Maybe not this time. It'll be weeks before she forgives me for disturbing the order of her classroom."

"Don't take it so hard, kid." Jeff punched my arm. "Scary Mary doesn't like anybody. Never has. Never will."

"Surely she likes somebody. Even Attila the Hun must have liked somebody."

"Nope. I have it on good authority that she only likes bugs and snakes and rabbits."

"A husband? A child? Surely somebody."

"Husband's dead. No one knows the particulars. It all happened years ago, but as far as I can find out no one suspected chloroform. No children. Nothing but snakes and bugs and rabbits."

I laughed. "I'll bet she'll like you."

"No chance," Jeff said with an exaggerated sigh. "None of the pretty ones ever do."

I looked at him closely to see if he was joking. "I didn't know Mrs. Lunsford qualified for that category."

"Take a good look at her," Jeff said seriously. "I'll

6

bet she was something when she was younger. She has good bones."

"That's what your mom keeps telling me." I put my hand to my cheek as if touching the bones could somehow help me believe it. "That I have good bones."

"Appreciation of beauty runs in the family."

"But you just said none of the pretty ones ever liked you, and I do. So I guess that puts me in the other category. The large category. The one with all the ordinary girls."

Jeff turned to me. "You, my dear, are in a category all to yourself."

Not sure I wanted to know if Jeff was making fun of me, I changed the subject. "Are you headed home?"

"I've got cross-country practice. We're going out to the golf course to run a few miles."

Jeff's always practicing something. His mom, Bev, accuses him of inventing things to do at school so he won't have to go home and do his chores, but she isn't exactly griping. Really she pushes him to be involved. Bev's always telling Jeff and me, too, if I happen to be around, that we need to take advantage of our high school years. To hear her tell it, the opportunities to be beauty queens and kings, track stars, cheerleaders, or basketball heroes are just hanging in front of us like apples on a tree and all we have to do is reach up and grab them.

She has more luck with Jeff than she does with me. At least he's out there running. Me, the best I can do is take pictures for the annual and make all A's. But A's don't impress Bev much. She expects that and more, so she always ends up smiling at me with that gee-I'm-sorry-but-you're-going-to-miss-all-the-fun look in her eyes.

Mom used to take up for me, but now Mom's so busy with Maddie that she hasn't got time to notice whether I'm running, cheering, or hiding in a dark corner. I don't really mind too much. Special talents like Maddie's require special sacrifices. By everybody. Besides, Mom couldn't help with my plans for overhauling the old Wendi Collins anyway.

Of course Tracy was willing to help. I told her all about what happened in biology class as we walked home.

"But that's fantastic." Tracy whirled around to grin at me. "It makes me almost wish I'd taken biology and had your luck."

"I didn't feel very lucky standing up there like a nut, a very red nut, while everybody laughed at me."

"Oh well, you have to take a few flies with the honey."

"What honey?"

"Why, Rod, of course. Just last week you were drooling over his picture in the annual when we were making out our list of prospects for the year."

"You said he was stuck-up," I reminded her.

"So maybe I was wrong. Who would you have been sitting behind if you'd listened and heard your name called, like a good little girl, instead of being goggle-eyed over Rod?"

"She didn't call out my name," I insisted. "But if she had, I'd have been behind Stewie Campbell."

Tracy let out a whoop. "Well, thank the saints for small favors. Or large ones as the case may be."

"Stewie's not so bad. He can't help it if he's smarter than the rest of the world."

"And wears glasses and only grew five-foot-five."

"A person can't help how he looks," I said automatically. My sermon was wasted on Tracy since she'd heard it too many times to really listen anymore. So I went on. "But at least with Stewie in front of me, I could have copied off his paper."

Tracy snorted. "You don't need to copy. You're probably the next smartest person in the world right after Stewie."

"Hardly. Don't forget Jason," I said. "But what I'd really like is to be witty and beautiful."

Tracy pushed back her hair. Naturally blonde, it lay in perfect curls and waves down on her shoulders. "And what I want to be is a voluptuous blonde."

"At least you've got the blonde part down right. And who knows about the rest? Maybe you aren't through developing yet."

Laughing, Tracy ran her hands down her sides. She was as slim as a pencil in her faded jeans, with hardly any curves at all. "Mama's pushing milk shakes at me, but so far it hasn't added an ounce anywhere. How about coming home with me and sharing one?"

"I don't need voluptuous." I wasn't fat, although I sometimes felt like I was when I stood next to Tracy. "Besides, I've got to go home and fix supper for Dad."

A look of sympathy flashed across Tracy's face. "Your mom off in the city with Maddie again?"

"Where else? They'll be home later, but it's a two-hour drive both ways and three hours with the coach."

Tracy hesitated before she asked, "How's she doing?"

"The coach says he should have started with her two years ago," I said, trying not to be bothered by

9

the question even though Tracy was supposed to be more interested in my campaign than in Maddie's. "But Mom says he's pleased with Maddie's progress. He says Maddie has great leaping ability and balance on the beam, but she needs to work on her tumbling runs for her floor exercise. She's not fluid enough. Of course she's so young yet."

"She's only ten, isn't she?"

"Almost eleven. But you need to start young to be really good in gymnastics, or so Coach Barton says, and he's supposed to be the best in this part of the South. Mom thinks it's worth the trip, and Maddie did seem to have improved a lot the last time I watched her working."

"I don't see how she does it." Tracy's look of wonder was replaced by a giggle. "Do you remember us trying to learn to do backflips and handsprings last year? You'd have thought our feet were set in concrete."

I tried to smile, but my lips wouldn't curl up. I was clumsy, ordinarily clumsy perhaps when compared to the average kid, but extraordinarily clumsy with Maddie dancing around the house, her feet floating above the carpet.

Still giggling at the memory of us falling on our backsides, Tracy said, "I don't believe I ever felt so heavy in my life. It's a good thing you strained your back and we had to give it up before we broke our necks or something."

"I'm glad you think it was so funny. I could hardly move for a week."

"Sorry," Tracy said with one last giggle as we reached our parting corner. "I'd like to see Maddie compete again sometime. She looks like she's lighter than air.''

''Like a butterfly.''

''Yeah, exactly,'' Tracy said with an amazed look. ''You always see everything in pictures. I guess that's why you're such a good photographer.''

When she said that, I forgave her for her awestruck admiration of Maddie. I liked the idea that I had an eye for good pictures. Anyway, I knew I might as well get used to people asking about Maddie because in a year or so everybody would be asking about my little sister, the Olympic hopeful.

As I walked back toward my house, a blue and black swallowtail butterfly floated across my path, and I wished I hadn't said Maddie was like a butterfly. Tracy might tell Maddie, and I didn't want Maddie to latch onto the idea. Butterflies were mine.

Ever since I could remember, I had loved butterflies. I'd spent hours chasing after them in the sunshine, and sometimes when the sun was bright enough and the breeze gentle enough I felt almost like I could float along with the butterfly from flower to flower.

All that was years ago, before Maddie started toddling. Still the memory warmed my insides, and my love of butterflies hadn't dimmed over the years. If I doodled, it was the shape of butterflies. Even when I was swimming, which is one of the few things I'm pretty good at, the butterfly stroke was my favorite. So although Maddie might be like a butterfly, butterflies were still mine, and I didn't want to share them with her.

The blue and black swallowtail flew ahead of me and settled on a white picket fence. As it fluttered its wings, gathering and turning loose sunshine, I wished for my camera. Reaching out, I gently touched the soft velvet of the butterfly's wings. It waved them lazily before lifting off its perch to float out of sight on the breeze.

When I went in, the house was empty and so quiet that I was glad when the refrigerator kicked on and began to hum.

I followed the sound out to the kitchen to see what Mom had left for me to cook, but there was nothing but a note propped on the table. Some of the words weren't much more than a scrawl, and I couldn't keep from smiling as I imagined how Mom must have been tearing around the house in a frantic rush to get off on time.

My smile faded when I read that Dad was going to stay late at the college for some kind of meeting. He's an English professor at the college in Campbellsville. I couldn't make out exactly what kind of meeting or when he'd be home, but it had to be late since Mom told me just to fix myself supper and not to worry about him.

I looked up at the cool, quiet kitchen and wished I'd gone home with Tracy. I considered walking over there even now. Tracy wouldn't care, but I'd been over there twice in the last week and more often than that to Jeff's. I looked out the kitchen window toward Jeff's backyard. His little sister, Kristy, was playing on the back steps. She's just a little younger than Maddie, and they used to play together all the time before Maddie's talent gobbled up all her free time.

Looking as lonely as I felt, Kristy sat among her dolls. I was starting out the back door when her father pulled into their drive, home from work. As Kristy ran to meet him, I stopped with my hand on the door.

They wouldn't care if I came over, but still I didn't go out the door. I was tired of feeling like an orphan showing up on everybody's doorstep.

I went back into the kitchen, crumpled Mom's note, and threw it into the trash. There were no dirty dishes in the sink, and the house was reasonably clean. There was nothing for me to do. My eyes caught on my notebook I'd laid on the table. At least in a few days I'd have homework to do. I shook my head at the thought that I was actually wishing for homework. The next thing I knew, I'd be wishing Jason would come banging down the steps demanding that I fix him something to eat before his lack of physical nourishment became fatal.

But Jason was off at college impressing all the girls with his good looks and extraordinary brilliance. Maddie was somewhere in the city floating above an exercise mat like a butterfly, and I was the only one here.

My eyes caught on my camera. Maybe it needed cleaning.

Chapter 2

Every time I saw Tracy after that we tried to hatch up some kind of fantastic scheme to take advantage of my-great-good-fortune-in-biology as Tracy put it. I told her there was no rush. I was sure it'd be weeks before I got tired of looking at the back of Rod's head.

Actually it only took one week, two days, and forty-two minutes. I mean there's just not much to look at on the back of somebody's head. By the end of the second day I had memorized the shape of his five freckles and knew the exact shade of his deep tan.

As the days passed I could practically see his hair growing. His shirts were a mind-dulling procession of football jerseys. My favorite was gold with the Brookfield Tiger stamped on it since the gold matched the sun glints in his light brown hair.

The only time Rod dressed up was the day of a football game, since the coach decided it might bring them good luck if all the players wore shirts and ties. Coaches will try anything for a win, and the Brookfield High football team hadn't had many wins during the last several years. Some people said Rod might just change that in the next two years, what with his way of popping up, sucking the ball into his hands, and racing into the end zone. Just another reason for girls to sigh over him.

On the third day in biology, I discovered that by scooting over just right I could sometimes see Rod drumming his fingers silently as Mrs. Lunsford lectured us. I could tell biology wasn't his favorite subject, and I told myself at least we had something in common. I wasn't overly fond of the class either.

As for Mrs. Lunsford, she hadn't forgiven me for messing up her seating order, and she was always springing the hardest questions on me. The fact that I knew the answers most of the time didn't seem to make her like me a bit better.

By the end of the first two weeks she had let us know exactly what we were going to have to do during the year to earn a good grade in her class. "You're in here to learn biology, not talk to your friends or daydream," she said with a piercing look back toward my corner.

I tried to look innocent as she informed us that we'd have several special projects to do during the year, the first of which would be an insect collection. Later there would be individual projects to prove some biological truth, and if we were good we might get to dissect earthworms and frogs before the year was over.

We could hardly contain our joy. Still none of it was news. Mrs. Lunsford had been teaching biology since before any of us were born, and she always did it the same way.

She was especially hard on the football players in her class. One day when a couple of them failed to turn in their homework, she let us all have her homework lecture. "I don't care how many football games, track meets, baton twirling contests or whatever you have. When I give an assignment I expect you to complete it fully and on time. If you do all your homework with a reasonable attempt at accuracy and without benefit of another student's paper and still fail all your tests, you might have a chance to pass this course. However, if you make all perfect marks on your tests and fail to complete your homework assignments, you might find yourself very disappointed with your final grade.''

Stewie Campbell, a braver soul than I, raised his hand. ''Would you fail somebody for not turning in his homework, Mrs. Lunsford? I mean even if they have a good excuse like football practice every day,'' he said with a sidelong glance over at Rod and a couple of other football players.

She stared at Stewie until he sank down low in his desk to try to get away from her eyes. Then she said, ''All students in this class are expected to complete each assignment.''

By the time three weeks were up, I was definitely bored with watching Rod's hair grow and had even considered tweaking his ear like Stanley Harris used to do mine back in fifth grade. At least then Rod would know I was back there behind him even if he did think I was crazy.

That Friday just before class let out, Mrs. Lunsford informed us that we could begin on our insect collections. She passed out a mimeographed sheet of which kinds of insects we were to get, how to kill them, mount them, and label them. When the bell rang she let us troop out of class by the way of the display case she kept in the back of the room.

Inside the case were two insect collections that must

have included every bug Noah took along with him on the ark. Alongside the flies, ants, beetles, and other striped and spotted bugs I didn't know existed were dozens of butterflies and moths, their beauty spoiled by the pins sticking through them.

On down in the case, her snakes were coiled in bottles of alcohol while a frog floated grotesquely in its jar. After that tour I was especially glad to get out of Mrs. Lunsford's room to where I could breathe the free air in the hall.

As usual Jeff was beside me. "See, what did I tell you about her bugs and snakes? She has them enshrined."

"You forgot the frog," I said.

"I was trying to." He made a face.

All the time we were talking I was edging closer to Rod, who was just ahead of us. Since it was football game day, he had on his white shirt and the deep blue tie that was just a shade darker than his eyes. I thought maybe if I could get close enough to him without being too obvious I could casually tell him I hoped he'd have a good game.

My heart was beating ten times a second, my hands were sweating where I gripped my book, and my mouth was sticky dry. But I was determined to speak to him. Three weeks of the year, my year when good things were going to happen to me because I was going to make them happen, had passed without anything happening. It was time I yanked up my nerve and started changing that.

I might have, too, if at that very moment Vanessa Tyrone hadn't appeared out of nowhere and with a little giggle latched herself to Rod's arm. She did it easily, without a moment's thought or hesitation, much less three weeks of planning. She knew Rod would just love to have her clinging to him, and from the smile on his face when he turned to say something to her, she must have been right. But then what boy wouldn't want Vanessa clinging to him.

Vanessa was a cheerleader and the kind of girl the class always picked for homecoming candidate or Snowball Queen or anything else to do with being pretty and popular. And she *was* pretty, with her delicate features and her golden blonde hair. Actually her hair wasn't a bit prettier than Tracy's, which I told Tracy all the time, but Vanessa had everything else to go with it, which I didn't tell Tracy.

Today, feeling especially mean, I looked at Vanessa's hips and legs and told myself she had fat thighs, but it wasn't so. The worst I could honestly come up with about her was that she had thick ankles.

As I slowed my steps, Vanessa laughed again, and the sound carried down the hall to Jeff and me. That should have been me laughing at whatever witty thing Rod had said. After all, it was my year. I had a list at home to prove it.

"Now there's a girl who has it all in the right places," Jeff said.

"She's not that great."

"I could say that about Rod, but I'm not sure you'd agree," Jeff said with a funny little smile.

"What makes you think that?" I asked cautiously.

"The way you've been drooling all over his neck for one thing." Jeff wasn't smiling at all now.

"I haven't been drooling over anybody."

"And I suppose you aren't going to the game to-night to cheer Rod on."

"I'm going out to support the team. The whole team."

"And I'm going out to support the cheerleaders. All of the cheerleaders."

"Do you have a crush on Vanessa?" I looked at him closely. "I mean it wouldn't be surprising. Half the boys in school are in love with Vanessa. Oh, to be a Vanessa."

Jeff laughed. "You don't really want to be a Vanessa, Wendi." He shook his head at me and laughed again as if the thought was ludicrous. "Besides, she's not my type."

"What is your type?" I asked. I used to think I knew about everything there was to know about Jeff, but lately I wasn't so sure. Along with his new muscles and the shadow of a beard on his cheeks, he'd changed.

So now I watched him curiously as he considered my question for a minute before he answered. "Every girl is different so I suppose it's not really fair to say type. But if I had to describe my dream girl, she'd be intelligent and witty with beauty but character as well in her face. Naturally she'd have a great figure, and last but not least she wouldn't be taller than me."

"You're not short."

"I'm not exactly basketball star material."

"No, you're a track star."

"I might be if I work at it." He looked up at the clock in the hall. "Which reminds me, I'd better get to practice. See you later." He took off up the hall in a controlled lope.

Jeff runs so easily, with natural rhythm and pace. His mom expects him to win the Boston Marathon someday.

That night was a beautiful night for a football game, with just a hint of crispness in the air. It was an even better night when we got our first victory of the year in the final moments of the game on a desperation pass to Rod, who caught it as he fell across the goal line. Everybody in the stands was on his feet, screaming, and Tracy and I were hugging each other. Of course out on the field Vanessa was hugging Rod. To keep from thinking about that, I grabbed my camera and focused in on a few of the kids up in the stands. All this happiness would make great candid shots for the annual.

By the time we got to my house, Tracy and I were both too hoarse to do much more than whisper, but we managed to whisper and giggle for most of the night.

The next morning Dad went with Mom and Maddie to the city, so when Tracy and I finally got up we were alone. As usual Mom's note was propped in the middle of the table. There were clothes in the washer that needed to be transferred to the dryer and doughnuts in the cabinet and juice in the fridge. When the roast thawed I could put it in the oven, and then if I had time I could run the vacuum.

I looked up from the note, glad Tracy was there. "They've already left with Maddie. Sometimes I think they forget they have another daughter."

"They left you a note."

"Outlining the chores for the day. That's a note for a maid, not a daughter."

"Stop feeling sorry for yourself, Wendi. I think it would be pretty neat having an Olympic champion for a sister."

"She's not an Olympic champion yet. She might

20

never be good enough and then all these hours will have been gone, for what?''

Tracy frowned. "If I didn't know you better, I'd say you were jealous of Maddie.''

"Why should I be jealous of Maddie? It's Vanessa I'm jealous of,'' I said, neatly changing the subject. Tracy was nearer to the truth than I cared to talk about.

"Vanessa's not that great,'' Tracy said.

"Rod Westmore thinks so.''

"Oh, I don't know.''

"No, of course not. He just lets her hug and kiss him because he can't politely refuse.''

"You might be right,'' Tracy said, grabbing at the idea. "Besides, last night was just a victory celebration. If you'd been out there on the field taking pictures for the annual, then you could have hugged him, too.''

"You know that Walter takes the football pictures. I'm supposed to cover cross-country.''

"Details, details. You've got a camera. You can take pictures of whatever you want to.''

"Sure,'' I said. "Walter would shove my camera down my throat if he thought I was pushing in on his territory. He's a strange boy. Besides, I can't see me running up and throwing my arms around a boy, any boy.''

"Well, I don't see why not. Vanessa did,'' Tracy said. "And Vanessa doesn't sit behind him in biology. You do.''

"A lot of good that does me. I could be a mound of stones for all he notices.''

"Maybe you haven't tried the right approach yet.''

"I did the pencil trick.''

"And he smiled at you, didn't he?"

"Not at me. Only at the lump of humanity behind him." I sighed over my juice. "Every day I risk bodily injury pushing down the up staircase to get to my seat in plenty of time so I'll be sitting right there in plain sight and wearing my best smile when he comes down the row to his seat. He's never, not once, looked at me. He just slides into his desk like it's the last one in the row." I looked up at Tracy. "And to tell you the truth, I'm getting a little tired of staring at the back of his head."

"Why don't you try asking him which page you're on?"

"In Scary Mary's class? She'd have my head."

Tracy's mouth tightened with aggravation. "You can't get attention if you're always hiding in the woodwork afraid of upsetting the applecart and making a teacher notice you."

"What good would it do to get Mrs. Lunsford yelling at me? You think that would impress Rod?"

"No, I'm not sure anything would. I'm about ready to decide maybe I was right about him to begin with. Maybe he is too stuck-up to notice us."

"I can't give up yet. I mean I've got eight more months of sitting behind him. Surely there's something, some way to get his attention."

Tracy sipped her juice. Finally she said, very seriously, "You're going to have to do something wild and crazy, Wendi. Something completely out of character for you. Something that will make the whole class notice you."

"What? Dye my hair green?"

Tracy giggled. "Maybe purple would be better."

Sighing, I stood up to clear the table. "I guess I'd

22

better get my chores out of the way so I can go out in the yard and catch bugs." I saw in my mind the collections in Mrs. Lunsford's case again. "Did I tell you about the beautiful butterflies somebody stuck pins through?"

"You told me. A dozen times already."

"There was a monarch and this velvety black and blue swallowtail and a luna moth that must have been as big as a bird. Prettiest moth I ever saw, and it was all stiff and dead."

"Why are you so worked up over a bunch of bugs?" Tracy asked.

"Not bugs. Butterflies."

"Okay, bugs with wings."

"You don't understand. Butterflies are meant to be free, not stuck on a board." Out the window I could see a dozen little yellow butterflies dancing in the yard. "I read once that butterflies fly only in sunshine."

"I knew you liked butterflies, but I didn't know you were this hung up on them."

"It just seems a shame to threaten their existence by collecting them for a biology project. Just think of the thousands, maybe millions of butterflies that will be killed if every high school biology student in the country has to collect insects."

Tracy jumped up from her chair. "That's it!" she cried. "I've had an inspiration."

"Oh no," I groaned as I looked at her warily.

"I know just the wild and crazy thing that you can do to make everybody at Brookfield High sit up and notice the real Wendi Collins."

"I'm not sure I want to hear this."

Tracy paid no attention. "We'll do a Save the Butterflies campaign," she announced, drawing the words out in the air. "Posters, the whole bit."

"You mean go up against Scary Mary?"

"Was all that talk about butterflies being free just a lot of empty words? Maybe you don't care about butterflies after all."

"Of course I do, but what can one person do?"

"For one thing, make Rod Westmore notice you're alive."

After Tracy talked out her inspiration, she went home. At first the words had bubbled up and over her lips like hot soda fizzing over, but then the doubts had set in. While Tracy has great faith in her inspirations, she needs a little cheering from the sidelines to keep her enthusiasm up, and I wasn't giving her any encouragement. Usually I egg her on because her inspirations can be great fun or at the worst interesting, but I just couldn't see how a Save the Butterflies campaign would do anything except get me in trouble with Mrs. Lunsford. Certainly not make Rod notice me.

After hurrying through my chores, I went out in the sunshine, which seemed as warm as summer even though the leaves at the very top of the big maple in the corner of the yard were touched with red. The bugs thought it was still summer, too. They were everywhere when I went out into the backyard with an old salad-dressing jar properly equipped with two alcohol-soaked cotton balls just like Mrs. Lunsford had instructed.

I caught a ground beetle and a gallinipper. Picking up a rock next to the garage, I nudged a roly-poly bug into my jar while the gallinipper made its escape.

Then carefully I trapped a bee sniffing a clover blossom between the jar and the top.

With the top securely screwed on I sat back in the sun and felt cruel while I waited for the bee to stop beating frantically against his glass death chamber.

I couldn't remember ever killing a bee on purpose. If one got around me it seemed just as easy to let it fly away as to swat it. I didn't even squash spiders when they got in the house. Instead I let them crawl up on a newspaper and then carried them outside, scared all the time that they might jump off the paper onto me.

I wished I couldn't hear the bee buzzing against the glass jar, but there were plenty of bees and such. Was I ready to sacrifice a few of them in the interest of a good biology grade?

Getting a good grade was important to me, which was why I hadn't cheered on Tracy's inspiration while she was all enthused over it. I wanted to get an A in biology.

I've always gotten A's. My parents expect it. Good grades are important to them, or they used to be. I just wasn't sure anything was important to them anymore except Maddie.

But me wanting to get good grades didn't have anything to do with Maddie or even Jason, though he'd never gotten all A's in spite of his brilliance. Or perhaps because of it, as he liked to say. He was always three steps ahead, a jump beyond what the teacher was teaching, and nobody could really blame him for not doing homework problems that he could do in his sleep.

No, every time I looked at all those A's marching down my report card in neat orderly rows, I felt like

I'd done something special. Maybe nothing extraordinarily special because lots of kids get A's, but a little bit special. If I got an F, it would be on my record forever, lining up with the A's. And no one would ever guess the bad grade was there because I didn't want to stick pins into butterflies.

Just then a butterfly drifted out of nowhere and began making a slow circle around me. It was one of those bright yellow and black ones, and it couldn't have picked a worse time to show up. I sat still and let it settle softly on my arm.

It was a bug with wings, I told myself as I studied its black body, but what a difference the wings made. As if reading my thoughts, the butterfly fluttered softly. How many days did he have here in the sunshine?

I reached out very slowly and caught the butterfly's wings, but when it struggled against my fingers, I turned it loose and watched it flit away. "That's right, butterfly," I whispered. "Fly away free."

I turned to pick up my jar. The bee was quiet now, not quite dead but close enough to realize the futility of fight. As I looked at the bee hunkered under the clover blossom, I started to unscrew the top to dump him out, but then I screwed it tight again. The bee would probably die now anyway. There was no sense flunking biology over a dead bee.

I'd stick every kind of bug Scary Mary ever thought of on my piece of Styrofoam. I'd boggle her mind with my assortment of spotted and striped bugs. I'd stay up till the wee hours of the morning finding names for them. But I wouldn't put any butterflies in my execution jar. After all, values were more important than good grades, weren't they? Values and beauty.

And who knew? Tracy might be right. The whole crazy idea might be just the way to make Rod Westmore notice I was alive. He probably didn't want to kill butterflies either.

By the end of the day I had three jars of bugs in various stages of dying. Some lay on the bottom of their jars with their feet up in the air while others still crawled about the slick sides of the jars, sure that somewhere there was a way to escape. A grasshopper thumped against the metal top of his jar.

I shoved all the jars out of sight in my closet and closed my ears to their frantic whirring as I began outlining my Save the Butterflies campaign by making a list of reasons butterflies should be exempt from capture.

The next day, after church, Tracy brought up the first hard question. "How about moths, Wendi?" She was helping me make a poster of different varieties of butterflies. "Are we saving them, too?"

"I don't know."

"Some moths are pretty." Tracy painstakingly added the last bit of color to a monarch. "Do they really eat up our clothes?"

"I think they lay their eggs in wool cloth or something like that."

"Eggs? I thought butterflies came from worms and cocoons and stuff like that." Tracy looked up at me with a startled expression. "I hadn't realized it, but we're on a campaign to save worms."

"Caterpillars."

"Whatever." Tracy waved her hand. "They really

27

can do a lot of damage. My pop is always spraying his garden for some kind of worm or other.''

"I suppose some of them can be pests." I put down my marker and stared at her. "Here I am ready to risk getting an F if Mrs. Lunsford doesn't like this idea, and the idea of Scary Mary liking this idea is about as likely as a live butterfly consenting to sit on my display to make it look good for a couple of hours, and you have to bring up caterpillars and worms."

"Sorry," Tracy said. After a moment she added, "Maybe you could just forget about the ugly little moths. Nobody would miss a few thousand of those. That way your grade will still be respectable, the butterflies will be saved, and Rod Westmore will ask you out."

I didn't see how Rod Westmore asking me out was a normal procession of the events Tracy had just outlined, but I didn't argue with the thought. Instead I thought about the drab little moths and butterflies that nobody would ever miss if they disappeared from the face of the earth. Finally I said, "I keep thinking that if I'd been a butterfly, I'd have been one of the little ugly ones. One of the expendable ones."

Tracy gave me a funny look. "Come on now, Wendi. This is just a little wild and crazy fun. If we spare a few pretty butterflies along the way, that's good, but don't get carried away."

"I'm not." But even as I said it, I started lettering a banner that read "Feed a worm. Give life to a butterfly."

Chapter 3

I left for school early the next morning after telling Mom I was doing a special project. She took me at my word and didn't even ask to see my rolled-up posters, but then mornings are always hectic around our house. And this morning there was some kind of new crisis with Maddie about deciding on music for her floor exercises.

At school Tracy and I waited until a few kids showed up to clutter the halls so we wouldn't be too conspicuous as we stuck our signs up.

I put the best poster in the middle of the bulletin board in the lobby area where the most people would see it. At the top I had lettered "Beauty flies with Butterflies." Then Tracy and I had covered it with pictures of the most beautiful butterflies we could find. At the bottom was the Save the Butterflies motto that we'd decided to use as sort of a trademark on all the posters and banners. Underneath that was my name in very small letters.

Tracy hadn't put her name on any of the signs. She said this was my wild and crazy thing, claiming she didn't want to take any of the credit, but now as we put the posters up, I wondered if it was blame she was avoiding.

29

Next to the poster of the butterflies I tacked up another poster outlining reasons for the Save the Butterflies campaign, which ended with the statement, "Butterfly lovers please sign below. Help keep beauty flying."

By the time the first bell rang there were already fifteen names on the sheet under the poster. In fact as Tracy and I slipped through the halls sticking up a banner here and there with bumper sticker slogans, a buzz of interest followed us around.

"By the end of the day everybody in Brookfield High will know who Wendi Collins is. I mean the real you," Tracy said with a big smile.

"Yeah," I agreed while the worry began to gather in a hard knot just to the right of my heart. "But will they forget again before the powers that be let me come back to school?"

"Stop worrying. They can't suspend you for putting up a few posters. People do it all the time. There's no rule against it in the student handbook."

I dreaded biology class all day, while the ripple in the halls grew steadily louder. At lunch the assistant principal, Mr. Andrews, had been studying the bulletin board, and I hadn't dared to go over to count the names on the poster. But even from across the lobby I could tell the paper was more than half covered. I wavered between being happy that the campaign was going over so well and wishing that I could just sink back into the wall and become old anonymous Wendi Collins again.

In biology every student awaited with anxiety and a certain relish the moment Mrs. Lunsford would mention the Save the Butterflies campaign. I was anxious, too, but in a different way. My throat was tight and my hands were shaking and my heart was trying to jump clear out of my chest. When she called on me to answer a question I nearly jumped out of my seat. She gave me an odd look but merely nodded when I stammered out the correct answer.

I knew then she hadn't noticed the signs and posters, as hard as that was to imagine. Then again maybe it wasn't so hard to imagine after all. She didn't think anybody would have the nerve to go up against her, and I was beginning to believe she was right. My nerve was shrinking to nothing there in her shadow.

Clasping my hands in my lap so my fingers wouldn't quiver, I made myself calm down. The ax wasn't going to fall today. I took a long, quiet breath and let it out slowly, and since there's just so long anybody can stay totally terrified, some of the trembling inside me stopped.

I decided to study Mrs. Lunsford while I had a chance. Surely there was a chink in her armor, some human soft spot that I could call on for mercy when she did discover my butterfly campaign.

I guess I'd been too busy studying the back of Rod's head to pay too much attention to how Mrs. Lunsford looked, but now the first thing I noticed was that she wasn't all that old. Her hair was still mostly dark brown with a few gray hairs to give it character. It was the way she wore it tucked back in a bun at the nape of her neck that made us kids think old. Her hair waved slightly, and I found myself wondering how long it was when she let it down.

She wasn't pretty pretty. But as Jeff had said, she did have good bones and she was attractive even though she wore absolutely no makeup. The thought shocked me, and I looked again.

31

I decided it wasn't her features that made us all believe she was ugly. Rather it was the way she held her mouth flat and stern, the way her chin could jut out and point out the slightest sound just like a finger, and last but not least the way her gray eyes could turn cold on any wrongdoer until said person wished to disappear from sight. I had the feeling she had total control of her expressions and used them the way another teacher might whack a desk with a ruler to restore order. Of course Mrs. Lunsford never had to restore order. She simply maintained it from the very beginning.

My stare was so intent that she suddenly turned her gray eyes toward me. When I looked down quickly, she asked, "Did you have a question, Miss Collins?"

I looked up, but not daring to meet her eyes again, I kept my eyes fastened on her mouth. "No, ma'am." I shoved the words out around the lump in my throat.

She stared at me a moment longer while the tension in the class practically thumped against the walls like a pulsing heart. Every student there knew I had put up the butterfly posters, and they were all waiting for Scary Mary's wrath to descend on me. As the moment lengthened I almost expected Stewie Campbell or some other kid wanting to get in good with Mrs. Lunsford to jump up and tell her what was going on. But the silence was complete, and finally the moment passed.

Class was almost over when Mrs. Lunsford riffled through some papers on her desk and then said sharply, "Mr. Westmore."

For the first time that day I took notice of the back of Rod's neck. He straightened up in his seat and, as far as I could remember, spoke for the first time in class. "Yes, ma'am?"

"You did not turn in your homework assignment."

"No, ma'am." He tried to sound casual, as though it meant very little to him, but from my vantage point there behind him I could see the red color creeping under the tan on the back of his neck.

"You have until the end of the week to make up the work for partial credit." She paused a moment before continuing. "Which I might remind you is better than a zero. You do want to pass this class, don't you, Mr. Westmore?"

"Yes, ma'am," Rod said meekly.

The bell rang at just that moment, and Rod sort of sank back in his seat. The color that had flooded the back of his neck began fading as he gathered up his books.

I could hardly believe that he had blushed. As I stood up to follow him out of the classroom, I smiled, because here was something else we had in common. Scary Mary could make us both blush. I could hardly wait to get home to put it on my list.

The first student was almost to the door when Mrs. Lunsford stopped us. "I hope you've all begun work on your insect collections. I have some specialized books if anyone needs help identifying some of the species."

A titter ran through the students that even Mrs. Lunsford's sternest look couldn't quite suppress. Nobody wasted any time getting out of the room into the hall.

Jeff grabbed my arm before I could ease over behind Rod. "What kind of crazy stunt are you trying to pull, Wendi?"

"It's not crazy. I just don't want to stick pins in butterflies," I said. "Do you?"

"You could just not put any butterflies in your collection without doing all this. You're openly flaunting her, you know, and she won't let you get away with it."

"I happen to believe in what I'm doing," I said staunchly. "Butterflies deserve to fly free on this planet without having to be subject to capture and torture by every biology student in the world. Even if each student only caught and killed one butterfly, can you imagine how many that would be altogether? The figures are mind-boggling."

"Why are you doing this?" Jeff was staring at me like I was demented.

"I just told you."

He frowned. "I don't want to see you get into trouble, Wendi, and mess up your grade point average over something this silly."

"It's not silly." I was more than a little disappointed over his reaction. And a little deflated. "Well, not entirely silly," I added.

Jeff was still looking at me in that strange way. "Why don't you just go rip all the posters down? Mrs. Lunsford hasn't noticed them yet. That way you can have your fun and maybe still stay out of trouble."

"You don't understand, Jeff," I said. "I don't want to see a bunch of dead butterflies stuck to Styrofoam! So I'm doing something about it."

"I don't believe this. What kind of idiot do you take me for anyway?"

"Jeff." I reached over almost timidly to touch his arm. "Why are you getting so mad?"

"I talked to Tracy at lunch. She told me what all this is really about, and now here you are spouting off about butterflies like you think I'm some kind of dope."

"What did she tell you?"

"I've got a meet," Jeff said over his shoulder as he turned away and started loping off up the hall.

"May your feet have wings," I called to him, but he didn't act like he heard me.

"Well, if it isn't the butterfly girl," a boy said beside me as I began walking up the hall after Jeff.

I looked around at Allen Mounts, another of the football players in my biology class and Rod Westmore's best friend. In fact Rod was there, too, right beside him, and both of them were really looking at me, Wendi Collins. I wanted to reach up and smooth down my hair, but I didn't. I just smiled at them sweetly and walked on.

"Wait up," Allen said, and together they pushed away from the wall and caught up with me.

Even though Rod still hadn't said anything to me, I looked at him instead of Allen and said, "Hi. Don't you have practice?"

"In a few minutes," Allen said. Allen was shorter than Rod and not nearly as good-looking. He'd been going with Mary Lou Carter for almost two years, but now he smiled at me with a little of that teasing charm he saved for all the other girls in the world besides Mary Lou as he said, "I'm sure you won't mind walking with me and Rod up toward the gym."

He looked over at Rod, who grinned sort of at me and sort of past me. It was a look that told all, as I realized Rod hadn't been entirely unaware that I had

35

been admiring his neck these past few weeks. Worse, he thought it was funny.

If I could have chanted a few words and disappeared, I'd have been out of their sight immediately. But since there was no way I could disappear, I grabbed at my pride, straightened my shoulders, and smiled at Allen. "I would, but I have to be getting on out to the cross-country meet."

"You're not on the team, are you?" Allen said.

"No, but I take pictures of the runners for the annual and keep time for them if they're shorthanded."

Rod spoke for the first time. "We just want to talk a minute." He put his hand on my arm to keep me from rushing off.

"Well, sure, I can talk a minute," I said.

Again Allen took over the talking. "You're making quite a stir with this butterfly thing. And while I don't want to stick bugs with pins any more than the next fellow, the fact is Scary Mary doesn't like football players. She thinks we're dumb whether we are or not."

"Maybe Wendi thinks we're dumb, too," Rod said softly, with his hand still warm and solid on my arm.

"No dumber than anybody else," I said.

Allen laughed a little. "We ain't exactly as bright as you and Stewie. At least Rod and me aren't. We could get all this stuff she puts on us if we had time, but the coach has a rule against missing practices."

"So?" I looked first at Allen and then at Rod. "What's that have to do with me or as far as that goes with butterflies?"

"We want to help you out with this bug thing, you know. I mean everybody likes butterflies," Allen said.

"Except Mrs. Lunsford," Rod stuck in.

Allen went on as though Rod hadn't spoken. "We thought maybe if we backed you up on this butterfly stuff you might help us out with our homework problems."

"How?" I was suspicious immediately.

"Well, you're a whizbang at all these questions and things Mrs. Lunsford's always asking," Allen said.

"She'd know if you copied," I said.

"Not if we went about it the right way," Allen said.

I shook my head, and Rod took his hand off my arm. He said, "I thought you wanted to be my friend, Wendi."

"We'd just get caught, and then we'd all get F's. You'd do better on your own."

"I'm surprised at you, Wendi," Allen said. "Nobody said anything about copying. We just wanted a little help."

"Sure, I'll help you," I said, positive that would be the end of that. "Come over anytime, and I'll be glad to help you with your homework."

Allen glanced at Rod, who shrugged and said, "Why not? Anything would be better than flunking and having to sit through another year of Scary Mary."

So at least I was a step ahead of Scary Mary, I thought. I didn't feel so special anymore.

Tracy popped out from behind a post up ahead of us. "Oh hi, Wendi," she said casually as if she hadn't been watching us all the way up the hall.

"See you later then, Wendi?" Allen said as he and Rod split off in the other direction.

"Sure. Anytime after seven," I called to them. Mom wouldn't be home from the city by then, but maybe Dad

would be home. I couldn't remember Mom saying anything about him having a meeting tonight.

When they were barely out of earshot, Tracy
jumped around in front of me where she could look
me straight in the eye and said, "What happened?"

"They said they might come over later." I tried to
be nonchalant, but Tracy saw through me. We both
burst into giggles.

"It's working then," Tracy said with a sigh of con-
tentment.

"Well, sort of," I admitted. "Actually they really
just want help with their homework so they won't
flunk, and I guess the butterfly campaign pushed me
up under their noses."

"And made them notice the real you just like I
planned."

"I'm not so sure about that. I told you they just
want help with their homework, and that's not exactly
what the real me had in mind."

"Give it time. They'll notice you in the right way
sooner or later."

"I'm afraid it's going to be Mrs. Lunsford who
notices me. In all the wrong ways."

"Did the thunder clap?" Tracy asked.

"Lightning has to strike first. Believe it or not, she
doesn't know about our butterfly campaign yet. Jeff
says I ought to take all the posters down now before
she sees them."

"What's Jeff know? He's just jealous," Tracy said.

"Jealous? What do you mean, jealous?"

"He doesn't want you getting interested in other
boys."

"You're crazy. Jeff and I are just friends. We've
always been friends."

38

"I know. I know. You're like brother and sister and all that nonsense," Tracy said wearily. "I mean really, Wendi, sometimes you can be so naive." And she gave me her superior look that meant I might know more about books, but she certainly knew more about boys.

"You're wrong," I said firmly. "But Jeff and I *are* friends, and I feel rotten when he's mad at me. How about going out to the cross-country meet with me? I've got my camera with me today."

"I'd rather watch the football team practice," Tracy said with a sigh as she glanced back toward the hallway where Rod and Allen had disappeared.

"Coach Buckley won't let anybody watch football practice," I said.

"You could take pictures."

"I told you that Walter takes the football pictures."

Tracy went with me, and I got Jeff's picture crossing the finish line as he won his first race. I hugged him and congratulated him, and he laughed and joked with us like always. Still something kept feeling different. Something I didn't want to feel different.

When I had set out to make changes in my life at the first of the school year that would make this year the year when special things finally happened to me, I hadn't planned to mess with the parts of my life that were good already.

Now it looked like one change was going to set off a string of changes like a line of dominoes falling down. I wanted to protect the butterflies so they could keep flying free in the sunshine. I didn't mind if in the process I made Rod Westmore notice I was alive. It wasn't quite so good that in the same process I would without a doubt get into trouble with Mrs.

Lunsford. Still while I wasn't too keen on the idea of getting a bad grade in biology, I had gone into the whole thing expecting that.

But I'd never even considered that any of it could touch the friendship between Jeff and me. That had always been something I could depend on no matter what else happened.

That night when Rod and Allen hadn't made an appearance at my house by seven-thirty, I was almost glad. Or I would have been if Tracy hadn't kept looking at the clock every five seconds and then at me as though I'd made the whole thing up.

Frankly I didn't believe Rod and Allen would actually show up until I opened the door at seven-forty, and there they were filling up the space on our small front porch. With my heart jumping clear up in my throat, I stared at them for a long minute before I could collect myself enough to ask them in.

Looking up from his book, Dad listened with a distracted smile while I introduced Rod and Allen. "They've come over to study," I said.

"Good," Dad said. "Kids your age don't always realize the importance of good study habits."

I jumped in before Dad could really get started on how kids didn't take advantage of the chances they had to learn. "We'll study in the kitchen if that's all right."

"Fine." Dad turned back to his book, unimpressed that two of Brookfield High's star football players were gracing his living room.

In the kitchen, I poured everybody a soda, and we got right to work. The homework wasn't hard. Rod and Allen zipped right through it when they finally realized I wasn't just going to give them the answers.

I was sure by the time they had finished writing out the last answers they would realize they could have done as well on their own with a little effort, but as Allen slammed his book shut and stood up, he said, "You were a big help, butterfly girl."

Rod smiled at me, and his blue eyes made my heart start fluttering wildly. He said, "Maybe we'll need you to help us again sometime."

"Sure, anytime." I hoped they didn't notice the excited little tremor in my voice, but they smiled at each other over the top of my head.

As they were leaving, Mom and Maddie came in. Maddie, who was usually tired and half asleep when she came home from the city, was jumping with excitement over seeing Rod's black Mustang in the driveway.

"Whose neat car out front?" she said as she bounced into the living room, wearing purple warm-ups over her pink tights. She looked cute, like Maddie always looked.

After I introduced Rod and Allen, they both spoke politely to Mom, and Rod asked Maddie, "Hey, kid, what you been doing? Cheerleading practice?"

Maddie bristled at once. "I should say not. I've been to the city to work with Coach Joseph Barton." When that didn't get any kind of reaction from Rod or Allen, she hurried on before I could think of a way to stop her. "I'm a gymnast, and by the time I'm your age I'm going to be a world champion and compete in the Olympics."

I sort of hoped Rod and Allen would laugh, but they just stared at her with their mouths open.

Dad looked up from his desk and called her down. "Madelaine," he said sternly.

41

"But I am." Maddie whirled to look at us all in turn as though daring anyone to deny it.

Mom, the last person I thought would ever try to deflate Maddie, said, "That may be so, Madelaine, but if so, it's a long time from now, and it's not good to be boastful."

"But it doesn't hurt to have a goal to work toward," I heard myself saying, hardly able to believe I was actually taking up for Maddie.

"Yeah, kid," Rod said. "Nothing wrong with wanting to be a champion. Your sis here is a butterfly champion." He poked Maddie on the shoulder lightly but smiled at me.

Maddie looked puzzled for a moment before she said, "Oh yeah, Wendi's great at the butterfly stroke. Did you guys go swimming or something?"

Allen and Rod just laughed a little at that and said their good-byes. I was relieved they hadn't gone into the butterfly thing since I wasn't quite ready for Mom and Dad to find out about my insurgence at school.

Running to the window, Maddie watched them take off. "I saw five cars just like that on the way to the city. And three red Corvettes, new ones, and one old white one and two Jaguars."

Tracy and I slipped back out to the kitchen while Mom began giving Dad a detailed account of Maddie's session with Coach Barton. As soon as we were alone, Tracy said, "Now that was an evening to remember."

I looked at her to see if she were being sarcastic, but there was an off-focus dreamy look in her eyes. "I thought maybe you'd think it was a little boring since all you did was watch us study."

"I guess it's all in who you're watching. You know,

Rod's cute and all, but Allen's got a lot of charm himself, don't you think?''

"Don't forget about Mary Lou.''

"Mary Lou? What's this got to do with her? Was she here?''

"In spirit," I said flatly. "She and Allen are practically engaged, or so the talk goes in the hallways.''

"Everybody talks.''

"And sometimes nobody listens." I hesitated, wondering how honest to be with Tracy. "Look, Tracy, he's not your type.''

"Oh, and I suppose Rod is your type.''

"At least he hasn't got a steady girlfriend.''

"What about Vanessa?''

"Vanessa would like to be his steady, but she isn't.''

"You're not either.''

"Not even close," I agreed with a laugh. "I'm his tutor.''

Tracy couldn't quite keep from laughing too. "Oh well," she said as she gathered up her things. "You've got to admit this Save the Butterflies scheme has been everything I promised you it would be." She grabbed the chair where Rod had been sitting just moments earlier. In her best dramatic voice she said, "Rod Westmore sat here. Here in this very spot. He laid his bare arm on this very table.''

"I'll never wash that spot again." I said solemnly.

We both started giggling again until Mom came back to the kitchen to see what was so funny. But of course we couldn't tell her. Not without talking for hours.

Chapter 4

The next morning I went over to see if Jeff wanted to walk to school with me and Tracy, but he'd already left. His mother answered the door, looking neat and efficient in her wine-colored suit, while behind her the kitchen was in chaos as usual. I sort of liked the clutter. It was a comfortable clutter, clutter that meant at least somebody was home long enough to make a mess.

"I would invite you in," Bev said with her quick smile. "But I'm afraid you might trip over something and sue me for maintaining a hazardous environment."

Because she worked for a lawyer, Jeff's mom was always joking about lawsuits. "That's okay," I said. "I haven't got time anyway. I just stopped by for Jeff."

Bev's smile disappeared. "Something wrong between you two?"

I'd always been able to talk with Jeff's mom about my problems, better than I could with my own mother, but I'd never had a real problem with Jeff before. So I just said, "I don't know. Maybe you ought to ask him."

She looked at me for another long moment, but

then she changed the subject by saying, "I saw you had company last night. Jeff said it was that Rod Westmore's car. He's the big football hero, isn't he?"

"Rod came over so I could help him with his biology homework."

"Biology, eh?" Bev raised her eyebrows. "I hope you're not studying sex education."

"Just the bees part. We haven't got to the birds yet."

Bev laughed, and I made a quick departure before I found myself asking her what to do about Jeff after all.

At school, Tracy and I went straight to the bulletin board. The paper was literally crammed with names.

"Everybody in school must have signed this." Tracy's voice was high and shrill with excitement.

"You don't see Mrs. Lunsford's name on there anywhere, do you?"

"No, but look." Tracy pointed at a name about midway down the list. "There's Mr. Andrews's name."

"Somebody else probably signed it," I said, even though I remembered seeing him reading the poster the day before. "He wouldn't have signed it."

"Can't adults be butterfly lovers, too?" Tracy studied the signature. "It looks like his signature in the school handbook."

The bell rang, and the hours raced past to the last class. The day went too quickly for me. I was so nervous as I found my seat in biology class and braced myself for the worst that I barely noticed when Rod came down the aisle, smiled at me, and mouthed a silent hi.

I half smiled back before my eyelids slid over to

45

where Jeff was taking his seat just across from me. He kept his eyes on his book and wouldn't look at me. If Mrs. Lunsford had attacked then, I would have just rolled over belly-up for the kill.

We spent the hour talking about plants and cross pollination. She didn't mention the insect collections until the class was almost over. First she made a production of sitting down behind her desk and closing her books.

Mrs. Lunsford's class was always quiet, but now as she sat there and stared at us the room was tomb-silent. Not one kid twisted in his chair or shuffled his feet or riffled a paper or page of his book. It was so quiet I could hear Rod breathing in front of me, and I was sure everyone in the classroom could hear my heart pounding. I wished fervently I'd taken Jeff's advice and ripped down all the posters before Mrs. Lunsford noticed them.

Finally she spoke. "It has come to my attention that there is a movement underfoot to undermine the learning experience of the insect collections I've assigned you. The only true way to establish a working knowledge of the many different species of insects is by capturing, observing, and labeling them correctly. I have given the assignment. I expect each and every student in my class to complete that assignment." She paused a moment before adding, "I will not deal lightly with insubordination among my students."

After another long moment of silence while I hardly dared to breathe, the bell rang. As I was gathering up my books, thinking maybe it hadn't been so bad after all, her voice cut across the room again. "Miss Collins, stay after class."

My hands became lumps of clay, and I knocked

my book off the desk. It hit the floor with a resounding thud in the still-quiet classroom although the other students were all out of their seats and headed out toward the hall.

Rod picked up my book and handed it to me. "Don't let the old bat get to you."

With his back to Mrs. Lunsford, he barely spoke loud enough for me to hear him, but again Mrs. Lunsford's voice cut through the air. "Remember the rules, Mr. Westmore. No talking until you leave my room."

"Yes, Ma'am," he muttered and made every effort to leave her room as quickly as he could.

She made me stand up in front of her desk for a full minute after the last student had filed out of the room. I would have thought it was ten minutes, but I could see the second hand on my watch as it crept slowly past each little mark.

When she finally looked up from the paper she was grading, her face was almost friendly, which made me even more nervous. "I hear you're a butterfly lover," she said.

I forced out a shaky, "Yes, ma'am."

"Why?"

I had my answer ready. "I've been reading lately about all the dangers that modern society is causing for the butterfly population, what with the spread of cities and the like. I feel we shouldn't do anything to add to their danger of becoming extinct."

"Extinct?"

"There are fewer butterflies now than there were ten years ago. If the trend continues, extinction of some of the species is possible."

"So you feel my insect collections are a threat to an endangered species. Is that right?" Her voice was

47

soft and agreeable while her eyes were growing hard and cold.

Swallowing hard, I said, "I'm not sure, but even if they're not, butterflies are still special and I don't think we should kill them without a good reason."

"Why are you really doing this?" Every bit of the friendliness drained from her face.

"I told you," I said weakly. "I think butterflies are special."

She dismissed my words with an impatient shake of her head. With a long, pointed fingernail she began tapping on a file folder that lay on the side of her desk. "I don't usually read the records that the school keeps on our students. I don't want to have preconceived ideas about the abilities of the students in my classes that might make me expect more out of some and less out of others than they might be able to reasonably produce." Again she tapped the folder. "However, in your case I made an exception."

She opened the folder and scanned the top page as if to refresh her memory. "I see Jason Collins is your brother. A gifted student who made the most of his abilities."

I groaned inwardly. Now I'd have to listen to the whole bit about how I'd do well to try to live up to the standard set by my wonderful brother.

But she didn't say any more about Jason as she went on. "And your academic career, as well, has been commendable up to this point. I find nothing here that would explain why you're attempting to disrupt the entire school over such a minor matter. More importantly, there is every indication that good grades and personal achievement are important to you." She looked at me pointedly before she added, "I'm sure we'd both hate to see your fine academic and conduct record spoiled.''

She waited for me to murmur yes ma'am, but I couldn't do it. With my insides quaking, I said, "I've broken none of the rules in the student handbook.''

"Each teacher has her own rules,'' she said firmly, fixing her sternest frown on me. "I want this nonsense stopped at once. Do you understand?''

"Yes, ma'am.'' I understood what she meant all right. My problem was getting her to understand about the butterflies and change her assignment.

Change the way Scary Mary taught biology? I could hear the ghost of every student who had ever sat in this room laughing behind me. Mrs. Lunsford didn't change. Her students changed.

When she dismissed me, I expected the hallway to be empty, but a few kids still stood around as if they were waiting to see if I had escaped Mrs. Lunsford all in one piece.

I supposed I had survived the first round still on my feet, but I wasn't sure I could go another round with her. She had all the advantages on her side. She was a teacher with the whole authority of the school administration behind her. Mr. Browning, the principal, would be sure to back her up in whatever she decided to do about my "insubordination" as she called it.

Me, all I had was a half-baked crusade to save a bunch of winged bugs, as Tracy called them. Was it really worth it? I could just say the heck with butterflies, rip down the posters, and tell Mrs. Lunsford that she was absolutely right. We ought to study butterflies by killing them and sticking them on Styrofoam. What did it matter if we were robbing the world of a bit of beauty?

Besides, there was no need in me lying to myself. No matter what else it had become, the whole idea of the butterfly campaign had been conceived by Tracy as a way of doing something wild and crazy enough to get Rod Westmore to notice I was alive. And in a way it had worked. I didn't need to get into any more trouble. I could slink back into my quiet little ordinary corner and throw in the towel. No doubt I could list a dozen reasons why that would be the sensible thing to do.

"I see she didn't eat you alive." Stewie Campbell fell in step beside me.

"Not yet," I said. "But she isn't happy."

"Scary Mary's never happy," Stewie said with a laugh. "I think what you're doing is great, Wendi. It's time somebody took on Scary Mary and let her know we won't take any more of her tyranny."

"Tyranny?"

"Sure, what else would you call it? She wants absolute control over every student, but you're showing her." A look of admiration flooded his face. "It took courage for you just to rush in and grab the bull by the horns like that."

"People who grab bulls by the horns can end up gored and bleeding to death."

Stewie laughed again as if the idea of me prostrate on the floor of the biology room bleeding to death was the funniest thing he'd ever thought of. "I didn't know you had such a sense of humor," I said a bit sourly.

"There's a lot you don't know about me," he said, his deep brown eyes intent on me.

A little quiver of something near panic went through me. "I guess that's true enough," I said lightly.

"I want to help you out."

"How? Are you going to grab the bull's tail?"

"Sort of. I hear you're having study sessions at your house to make sure we all get such great grades on our tests and homework papers that Mrs. Lunsford will have to pass us even if we don't murder butterflies."

I wasn't sure who had told him we were having study sessions, but if it had been Rod I didn't want to call him a liar. So I halfway nodded and said, "Sometimes it's easier if a bunch study together."

"I don't need to study." Stewie wasn't boasting, just stating a fact. "But I could come over and help others."

"That'd be great, Stewart," I lied. "But I don't think anybody is coming over tonight."

"Oh yes, they are. I heard some of the kids talking about it after class. You must have a great mother to let so many kids pile in on you like this."

"So many kids?" I said faintly. "How many kids?"

But Stewie was already halfway down the hall and didn't answer me.

Jeff was waiting for me at the door. "You'll be late for cross-country practice," I said with a quick glance up at the hall clock. I was surprised but glad to see him there. So glad that I wanted to hug him, but of course I couldn't. Not since the ground had sort of shifted under us, changing our friendship.

"So I'll have to run an extra mile," Jeff said with

51

a shrug. "I couldn't leave till I knew you were all right."

I smiled as warmth spread through me. "Of course I'm all right. You didn't think she would bodily injure me, did you?"

"I wasn't sure." He looked at me closely, as though he expected me to sprout bruises any second. "What did she say?" he asked as he began walking toward the track.

"She isn't a butterfly lover." I sighed and fell in beside him. "I think maybe I'm in a lot of trouble if I don't just give it up now."

"Then give it up."

"You really think I should?" I looked over at Jeff, who didn't meet my eye. "I mean everybody in school is really into this."

"They're just having fun with this, that's all."

"What do you mean? Can't other kids like butterflies as much as I do?"

"Come off it, Wendi. The other kids just want to upset Mrs. Lunsford. It hasn't got anything to do with butterflies."

"I don't believe that. They wouldn't take a chance on getting a bad grade just for fun."

"And you would?"

"Surely she won't fail me for the whole year just because I don't put a butterfly in my insect collection."

"You're sure about that?" Jeff said.

"Not really. She was pretty upset. She said I was undermining her authority."

"You could quit now and things would settle back down. That might be good enough for her." He looked over at me and then quickly away. "I mean the scheme's already worked. You've got Rod interested."

I could have told Jeff that Rod wasn't interested in anything but my homework, but I didn't. Instead, with a little laugh, I said, "Stewie, too."

"Stewie?"

"He's coming over to help me conduct my study group tonight. The way he tells it half the class is going to be there."

When Jeff just kept staring at me as if I had two heads, I went on. "I didn't know butterflies had such power."

"Maybe I should come over, too," he said finally.

"Sure, come ahead. The more the merrier. Of course Mom and Dad may kill me. Neither of them is going to be home tonight."

Dad still wasn't home from his meeting when six or seven kids showed up at the same time that night, including Rod and Allen and Stewie. Of course Tracy was already there. She wasn't about to miss sharing the fruits of her inspiration. Then Mary Lou and Vanessa showed up. They had biology at a different hour, but the homework was pretty much the same.

Of course they didn't really come for help with their homework. They came to protect their interests, and by the time there were kids sitting on every available chair in the kitchen with a few spilled out on the floor I couldn't have cared less. Vanessa pulled her chair over close to Rod's to share his book. Her blonde hair drifted down and lightly brushed his hand as they leaned over the book together.

Stewie made a great teacher. He had a way of explaining things so that the densest person could catch right on. As he talked, a certain excitement lit up his face, and you forgot about his glasses and that he was short and skinny. Once I even grabbed my camera and took a quick shot of him without him noticing.

Jeff didn't come over until after all the kids had closed their books and were talking about going en masse to the park to catch bugs that weekend.

"You got room for one more?" Jeff said from the back door. He peered around the room and took in Vanessa scooted up close to Rod. "Not working out so well tonight, huh?" he whispered to me as he came in.

"Come on in, Jeff," Allen called out to him. "Mary Lou can sit in my lap, and you can even have a seat." Allen scooped the unprotesting Mary Lou up and into his lap. She leaned back against him as though he were an old, familiar chair.

Jeff went past me into the room, acknowledging the greetings thrown to him. They all liked him, I thought, and then wondered why I was surprised. A person didn't have to be a football hero to be popular. Even Stewie had been likable and part of the crowd tonight.

"So we'll all meet at the park around ten Saturday," Stewie said after Jeff sat down.

"To catch bugs," one of the kids over in the corner added for Jeff's benefit.

"But no butterflies," Rod said very seriously. His eyes came up to meet mine, and again there was that smile I wasn't sure about. Was he smiling with me or at me?

Vanessa grabbed at his attention. "You know my name means a kind of butterfly."

"You don't say, Essie," Allen said. "And we thought Wendi here was the butterfly girl."

"What kind of butterfly are you, Vanessa?" Mary Lou asked.

"I don't know." With a little pout, Vanessa turned to Rod. "What kind do you think I am, Rod?"

"Don't ask me. I'm not the butterfly expert. Wendi is."

All eyes turned to me, and I sort of smiled and said, "I'm sure you're a monarch, Vanessa."

My answer pleased her, and you could almost see her glow under the attention. And she was pretty, with her every hair properly curled and her eyes highlighted with makeup to make them look even bigger and bluer. I didn't like thinking about what I must look like in contrast.

Allen was still looking at me. "What kind of butterfly are you, butterfly girl?"

"I don't know. Maybe I'm still a caterpillar."

Rod looked up and laughed. This time I was sure it was with me, but Jeff leaned back in his chair with a frown.

All at once everybody started leaving as if they'd just remembered the time. Vanessa and Mary Lou managed to go outside right in front of Allen and Rod.

Tracy came over and whispered, "Stewie's giving me a ride home."

"Stewie?" I didn't even try to keep the surprise out of my voice.

"I've been watching him tonight. Actually he's kinda cute, and he's promised to help me with my math."

As Stewie held the door for Tracy, he kept his eyes fastened on her like she was the greatest thing since sliced bread. Giggling, Tracy flashed her eyes at him.

When I looked around, Jeff was the only one left, and I was relieved that the rest of them had cleared out before Mom or Dad got home. Of course I'd have to tell them I'd had company, but at least they wouldn't have the shock of coming in and finding twenty-some-odd kids crammed into the kitchen. I began picking up dirty glasses and carrying them to the sink.

Jeff pushed the chairs back into their proper places. "Why'd you say that, Wendi?" he asked.

"What?"

"That you were a caterpillar. There wasn't any reason for you to put yourself down like that."

I stared into the darkened window over the sink at my soft reflection and said, "I was just telling the truth. I may be a butterfly someday, but not yet. I'm still developing whatever kind of person I'm going to end up being."

"And you think Vanessa isn't?"

"I don't know. She's already pretty enough to be any kind of butterfly she wants to be. I just said the first thing that came to mind." I began filling the sink with water.

"Do you know what your name means?" Jeff asked.

"I looked it up once, and I think it means wanderer, someone who searches for violets in the snow." I looked at Jeff's reflection in the window next to mine. "Do you think I'll ever find any?" I meant to make him smile, but he didn't.

"Maybe," he said solemnly. "The trouble is not only knowing where to look but recognizing what you've found when you find it."

"That's the way it is when you take pictures, but I know what violets look like. I've just never seen any blooming in the snow. But that would make a great picture, wouldn't it? Violets with snow all around them.''

"Yeah, I suppose.'' Jeff pushed the last chair in place. "I've got to go home.''

I looked around at him and smiled. "I'm glad you came over, Jeff,'' I said. "Thanks.''

He looked at me as if I'd said something especially odd, and I suppose I had. I'd never thanked him for coming over before.

"Yeah, sure,'' he said as he slipped out the door.

Washing the glasses slowly, I watched for the light to spill out when he opened his back door to go inside. Then Mom and Maddie got home, and I told Mom about the kids coming over to study.

She wasn't upset. She just said, "It might be better if you picked nights your father was going to be at home.''

"I didn't exactly pick tonight,'' I started to explain, but she wasn't really listening. Deep frown lines creased her eyes, and I asked, "What's wrong? Did Maddie sprain something?''

"No, nothing important.'' Mom rubbed her forehead. "I guess I'm just tired, and Madelaine still hasn't decided on her music. The deadline's next week.''

"Just pick out something for her,'' I said, cross that once more Maddie's affairs were more important than mine.

"I would,'' Mom said with a heavy sigh. "But Coach Barton says it's extremely important that Madelaine makes her own choice and that she loves the music because she's going to have to be working with it for at least a year. Maybe longer.''

"She'll think of something." I couldn't really worry about Maddie. I had enough to worry about myself, what with butterflies and Mrs. Lunsford and Rod and Jeff.

Chapter 5

On Saturday the sun streaming in my window woke me. After dressing in my favorite blue shorts and the new white top Mom had brought home from the city, I ran down the steps with a tingle of excitement growing inside me. I had something to do. Something special.

When I went into the kitchen and saw Mom, I looked up at the clock; I knew I hadn't gotten up that early. She should have been gone hours ago. "What's going on?" I asked.

Mom turned from the stove to smile at me. "Good morning, dear," she said. "I was just trying to decide whether to make pies or a cake for supper."

"Why aren't you in the city with Maddie?"

"Jason came in late last night, and since it's been more than a month since he was home, I decided to let Madelaine take the day off."

"Jason's home? That's great," I said. "Where is he? Still in bed, I suppose."

Mom nodded while that special smile she reserved for Jason lit up her eyes. I decided it had something to do with a mother and her only son since I'd seen Jeff's mom look at him the same way.

"But what about Coach Barton?" I asked. "I

thought he said Maddie couldn't miss practice unless there was an earthquake or something.''

"Actually he wasn't as upset as Madelaine. She has gotten so wrapped up in all this that she hardly knows what to do with herself when she's not practicing. Of course she has to be that way if she really wants to be good, but sometimes I wonder if we're doing the right thing pushing her like this.'' Mom's face looked drawn and tight, with a few new wrinkles, as if she'd aged a year since the last time we'd talked on Saturday morning.

"Where's Maddie now?''

"Your father took her to the Y to practice.''

"Did you make her go?''

"No. I told her to sleep in.''

"Well, see, then. Maddie doesn't need anyone to push her. She wants it herself.''

"But I want it, too. She's so good, Wendi. She makes me so proud that sometimes when I watch her I don't think I'll be able to stand it if she doesn't win.''

"She always wins.'' I didn't want to talk about Maddie anymore. "How about Jase? What's he up to?''

I was sorry I had asked as soon as Mom answered. "He may get to go overseas to study this summer. He's being considered for some kind of special grant.''

That's the way it always was with Jason. He had a great bit of news every time he came in from school. He'd been elected an officer in his fraternity. He'd been picked for the lead in the drama department's play. His poem was being published in the school magazine. He'd hung the moon and polished the stars.

It made catching or not catching butterflies sound a little tame in comparison, but I wasn't about to let them spoil my day. No matter what, I was going to hang on to the feeling of something special about to happen that I'd gotten up with.

"Cake." I grabbed an apple and my camera and started out of the kitchen. "Jason likes cake best."

"But you like pie," Mom said.

"Cake's all right." I let the door slam shut behind me.

I was glad to be outside in the sunshine. All week long I'd lived so in dread of Mrs. Lunsford and what she was going to do to me that I hadn't even noticed whether the sun was shining or not. But I had survived a whole week of rebellion, and even though the principal had made me take down my signs on Wednesday, no one seemed too worried about the whole thing. Except of course Mrs. Lunsford. After calling me into his office, Mr. Browning had simply given me his general all-purpose "respect your teachers" lecture and warned me to clear all posters with him before I put them up from now on.

Actually I was willing to let things cool off a little. But the kids had ordained me the butterfly girl, and they weren't about to let me forget my new title even if I wanted to. Save the Butterflies had become something of a rallying cry in the halls of Brookfield High before the week was out. The braver kids liked to whisper it whenever they saw Mrs. Lunsford in the corridors. As far as I knew she never gave any indication that she heard any of the whispers in spite of the fact that she'd already proven she had acute hearing in class.

Neither did she let her eyes stray to any of the butterflies or slogans that kept appearing like magic on the corridor walls, some with new slogans that had nothing to do with butterflies. Down with Scary Mary and Scary Mary Can't Scare Us became as common as my Save the Butterflies.

Thank goodness Mr. Browning had believed me when I told him I hadn't put up any of the new posters when he'd called me into his office again on Thursday.

He leaned back in his chair, folded his arms, and stared at me. "I believe you, Wendi," he said finally. "But that doesn't change the fact that you started all this nonsense, and therefore in a way all the posters that are up in the hall now are still your responsibility."

"I didn't tell anybody to put up a poster," I said. "Especially the ones about Mrs. Lunsford. I wouldn't do anything like that."

"Maybe not, but you could tell them not to put up any more."

"You think they'd listen to me?"

"They listened to you before." Mr. Browning leaned back in his chair and tapped his fingers together as he studied me. "Look, Wendi, I realize this whole thing has probably blown up lots bigger than you expected. Nevertheless I can't let it get out of hand."

"I'll take down the signs," I offered.

"And recant your position," he ordered.

"I can't." I stumbled over the words while my heart began pounding inside me. "I mean the other kids can do what they like, but I can't put a butterfly in my insect collection. And I don't think I could tell the others to."

The way his eyes narrowed on me was enough to make me tremble. "Nobody's going to miss a few butterflies, Wendi. Not that I think butterflies are exactly what all this is about," he said. "Just take down the posters and don't put up any more."

My mouth was too dry to answer. So I just nodded, and when he said I could go, I left as quickly as my rubbery legs would carry me. It took me almost an hour after school that afternoon to tear down and scrape off all the signs.

It was a relief when football posters took control on Friday. Still I wouldn't say butterflies were forgotten, as half the posters were sporting butterflies in some shape or fashion. One copied that old Muhammad Ali slogan by stating the Brookfield Tigers "floated like butterflies and stung like bees."

And Friday night they did. I never saw or heard so much enthusiasm running through the crowd, and the team responded with two interceptions. Rod had three long runs, one a seventy-yard return on a kickoff. It was the first time Brookfield High had won two games in a row for three years.

The enthusiasm carried over to the next day, and when the kids began showing up at the park, everybody was in great high spirits. By the time Rod pulled his car into the lot, a whole pack of kids were waiting to pounce on him.

"Hey, that was some game last night, Rod," one of the kids said, while another slapped him on the shoulder.

"You were just great, Rod," somebody else said. It was a girl's voice, and even from my station over on one of the swings, I could hear the quiver of breathless admiration in her voice that covered more than how Rod had played football the night before.

The sound of the girl's voice made me cringe a

little. I had planned to congratulate Rod on his game myself, but I decided to stay on my swing, swaying it back and forth and holding my head and arms just so in case Rod happened to glance my way.

Rod seemed a little embarrassed by all the fuss as he shrugged off their compliments. "I got a lot of help from Allen and the other guys."

Looking at Rod, I decided I was beginning to like him as more than just a great-looking guy. He surprised me by actually looking my way and smiling when the crowd of kids thinned out around him.

Instead of walking up to the gate and into the park, Rod casually lifted himself up over the fence that separated the picnic area from the parking lot and landed as light as a cat on the other side. He moved toward me with the easy rhythm of a natural-born athlete. Watching him, I thought of soda and jeans commercials on TV where everybody always looks special.

When he stopped in front of me, I blurted out, "Have you ever thought about being a model?" A rush of color burned my cheeks as soon as I let the words out.

Rod just laughed a little. "Nope. I was thinking more about football."

"You want to be a pro?"

"You look like you think I'd have better luck in the modeling department."

"Not really," I said quickly. "It's just that no one from Brookfield has ever gotten as much as a full college scholarship for football."

"Then I'll be the first. I'm good," Rod said flatly with no false modesty. "Maybe not as great as the kids would like to think, but good enough. And I'm getting better all the time. By the time I finish my senior season some colleges are going to want me, and then eventually I'll be in the pros.''

"You sound like my sister when she says she's going to the Olympics.''

"Maybe she will.''

"She has a chance. Maybe someday I'll be watching both of you on television.''

"What about you, butterfly girl? What are you planning on doing with your life? Become an entomologist or something?'' He asked it with that smile I was never quite sure of.

"How about a model?'' I said as I stood up.

He laughed again, and I knew I'd scored another point with him. He was about to say something when Vanessa appeared out of nowhere and threw herself at him. She looked gorgeous in a red scoop-neck top and short white shorts that showed vast vistas of honey-brown legs. Her thick ankles were out of sight under cute little tennis socks.

Rod casually hugged her up against him the way one might stroke an enthusiastic kitten who was begging for attention. Still Vanessa bubbled with pleasure, and listening, I wasn't quite sure I didn't hear her purring.

I turned away from them. "Is everybody ready to catch bugs?'' I called. "Did you bring your jars?'' I held up mine.

"You mean the old execution chamber,'' Stewie said.

I wasn't surprised to see Tracy right there beside Stewie. Since that night at my house, it had been Stewart this and Stewart that every time I was around Tracy, which hadn't been as much as usual. She didn't have time to come over because Stewart was tutoring her in math, a task that had been mine up until now.

A few minutes later, after we had split into small groups to begin hunting insects, Tracy fell in beside me. "Isn't it a gorgeous fantastic super wonderful day?" she said.

"It's pretty. A great day for taking pictures." I pulled my camera up and took a picture of a couple of kids chasing a gallinipper.

"You're supposed to be catching bugs, not taking pictures," Tracy said.

"Oh, I don't know." I took a couple more shots. "The annual probably could use some bug-catching pictures. It might make an interesting special-interest spread. After all, Mrs. Lunsford has been making students catch bugs for years and years."

I dropped my camera back down to hang from the strap around my neck and looked at Tracy. She didn't act like she'd heard a word I'd said as she stared over at Stewie.

"Did you come with Stewie—I mean Stewart?" I asked.

"Who else?" She sighed. "He's just so sweet."

"Sweet? Stewie sweet?"

"You just don't know him well enough." Tracy's mouth stiffened out in a hard line.

"I'm sorry, Tracy. You're right. Stewart's very nice."

She looked at me closely, but my sincere look must have convinced her. She smiled again. "He thinks I'm exquisite. His very word. He asked me to go to the sock hop next week."

"That's great." I pushed enthusiasm into my voice.

"You honestly think so?"

"Of course I do. I'll come over and help you get dressed," I said as I pounced on a hapless cricket and stuck it in my jar.

Tracy watched the cricket bang against the glass for a minute before she said, "My mother believes killing black crickets is bad luck."

"Just shut your mouth. I'm not about to start a Save the Crickets campaign."

"All right. All right." She giggled and stooped down to lift up a rock. Another black cricket shot out. "Here, you want another one?"

"I could keep it for Jeff."

"Where is Jeff?" Tracy looked around.

"He had a meet." I grabbed the cricket, which jerked free minus one of its legs and scooted back under the rock. When Tracy started to pick up the rock again, I said, "Let it go."

"You're too softhearted." Then, as if she'd never talked about anything else, she said, "But you'll be coming to the sock hop, too."

I made a little face. "Not by myself."

"Maybe Rod will ask you. I saw you two talking when we got here."

"Big deal. So he knows I'm alive. Your scheme worked as far as that goes. But as for him asking me to the sock hop, I think that's expecting too much of a Save the Butterflies campaign."

"Oh, I don't know. It's already got us more than we figured on."

"Or bargained for. From the way Mr. Browning looked at me Thursday I think I'm that close to getting a rest from school altogether." I held up my fingers about an inch apart.

"Oh, quit worrying so much, Wendi. He won't

suspend you.'' Tracy threw her arms out toward the sun and trees and then wrapped them around her body as though she were embracing the world. ''Just let go and be truly wild and crazy for once in your life. Mr. Browning isn't going to kill you.''

''Maybe not. But how about Mrs. Lunsford? I'm beginning to think wild and crazy isn't my style. Ordinary is much easier on the nerves.''

''But not near as much fun.''

It didn't take very long for all of us to get tired of chasing bugs, but the hunt was successful. When everybody started gathering back at the picnic tables, the jars were crawling with every kind and shape of bug imaginable.

Except my jar. I'd been too busy snapping pictures of the other kids catching bugs to catch bugs myself. I only had the cricket that was still banging against the sides of the jar and an odd little beetle. When nobody was looking, I unscrewed the top and let the cricket bounce away. The little beetle tumbled out behind him. I watched him trundle away to safety under a leaf before I hid my empty jar.

Nobody noticed my missing jar, but they made sure I got a good look at theirs so that I could see there were no butterflies. I had seen about all the frantically dying bugs I cared to see in one lifetime when somebody saved my sanity by producing a volleyball.

After taking a few pictures of the kids warming up by knocking the ball back and forth, I stashed my camera in a safe place as they began dividing up into teams.

Stewie and Tracy were on the same team, but Rod and I were on opposite sides of the net. I loved playing volleyball almost as much as I loved to swim, and as I watched Rod shake his muscles loose and get ready to serve, I knew he would be good at the game, too. In my head I marked up volleyball as another thing we had in common. The list was getting much longer than I'd ever dreamed it would.

Early in the game Rod spiked a couple of balls between Vanessa and me. Each time Vanessa jumped back away from the ball with a little shriek. "Now Rod, you're just being mean," she said with a pouting look in his direction as though no one else were playing.

"You think you could hit back an easy one, Essie?" Rod laughed indulgently.

"I don't know," she said. "That old ball stings my hands." She held up hands that couldn't be stinging since she hadn't touched the ball yet.

Allen went over and rubbed her wrists and showed her how to hit the ball if it came her way again, which we all knew it would. That's the way to win in volleyball—by hitting it to the other team's weakest player. We were doing the same by giving poor Tracy and Stewie a workout on the other side. Tracy wasn't usually so inept, but I got the feeling she didn't want to outplay Stewie, who looked as though he'd never seen a volleyball before in his entire life.

Finally Rod got a chance at the ball again when Vanessa and I were on the front line. He gave it a soft tap that he thought would carry over to Vanessa, but I'd gotten tired of their private game. Besides, I'd never yet let an easy ball like that go by without shoving it down the other player's throat. I jumped up in front of Vanessa and rammed the ball back at Rod.

He was too surprised to even make an effort to hit the ball. Allen laughed behind me. "Well, well," he said. "Looks like our butterfly girl can sting like a bee."

Rod didn't so much as smile as he looked at me, but it wasn't a bad look. Rather, a considering look, as if he were finally seeing me. After that the private game was between us as he slammed the ball at me every chance he got. Some of them I returned, and some of them I didn't.

Caught up in the game, I didn't give a thought to how I looked and only worried about returning the ball when it came my way. With Allen on the front line, we won the game on my serve.

As everybody began breaking up to find their insect jars before heading home, Vanessa looked at me and said, "Gee, Wendi, I didn't know girls could sweat like that."

Standing there without a hair ruffled out of place and only a bit of a flush in her cheeks to add to her good looks, she might have been on an air-conditioned court for all the sweat she showed.

I knew what I must look like in comparison, but I didn't give her the satisfaction of seeing me tuck in my shirt. I only grinned as I picked up my camera and said, "It's fun. You ought to try it sometime."

Allen came to my aid then. "She's right, Essie. You don't make much of a volleyball player."

"I suppose not," she said with a delicate little sigh. "I guess I'm not made that way."

Allen laughed. "I guess not." He came over and threw his arm around me like I was one of the boys. Our sweat mixed as he said, "Great game, kid."

"Sure," I said. "You, too."

"We'll have to play together again sometime. Maybe on opposite teams. I like a challenge."

"Anytime." I turned away from him. I wiped my forehead on my arm while I wished for my sweatbands and then vainly tried to push my hair back into shape. Still I didn't tuck in my shirt.

Tracy grabbed my arm and pulled me roughly to one side. "What's the matter with you?"

"I'm hot for one thing," I said, wiping my forehead again. "Thirsty for another."

"You know what I mean. Why in the world did you spike that ball at Rod?"

"I won the point, didn't I?"

"It's according to which point you're talking about." Tracy shook her head as if I were a hopeless case. "Honestly, Wendi, sometimes I wonder about you. You should have played off. Boys don't like girls who beat them."

"I didn't beat him. My team beat his team and your team. I might ask what's the matter with you. You acted like you'd never seen a volleyball before."

"You think I want Stewart to think I'm some kind of female jock?"

"Oh, come on, Tracy. Surely Stewie's liberated enough to admire a little athletic ability in a girl."

"A little ability maybe, but not more than he has."

"I surely didn't show more athletic ability than Rod."

"You didn't exactly look like Vanessa."

"Thank goodness," I said, but Tracy went on as if I hadn't spoken.

"And look at you. You're a mess."

"Maybe, but I helped my team win and I didn't pretend to be something I'm not just to impress some boy. I'll leave the helpless female role up to you and Vanessa."

For a second I thought Tracy might smack me, but instead she turned on her heel and stalked away. I started after her to tell her I was sorry, but Stewie reached her first. The stiffness in her back just melted away as she leaned up against him and laughed.

Turning away, I headed out of the park. Why should I be the one to apologize anyway? I hadn't done anything or been the one who had changed. In spite of all my plans at the first of the year, I was still the same ordinary girl I'd always been.

It was Tracy who was changing, molding herself into the kind of girl she thought Stewie or any boy would like. And it could be that she was right, since she was getting to ride home with Stewie in his father's classic '57 Chevy. And what was I doing? Carrying an empty jar because I was a tenderhearted idiot, I was walking home with sweat still running down my face and my shirttail hanging out while my mouth felt like cotton. My special day had flopped like everything else I tried to do. At least today had been an extraordinary flop. Nothing ordinary about it.

Tracy didn't even glance over at me as she and Stewie passed.

When I thought all the kids from the park had passed, I tucked my shirt in and began walking faster. I'd gone a couple of blocks when a car slowed behind me and tooted its horn. Rod was sliding along beside the walk in his black Mustang. "Hey, how about a ride?" he asked.

The color heated up my face again, and I hoped Rod would think I was still flushed from the volleyball game. "Sure, why not?"

He was pushing open the door. "Get in before somebody sideswipes me."

After I got in, he shoved through the gears before he glanced over and said, "That was some spike you rammed at me."

"You made me a little mad with the ones you'd pushed my way earlier."

He laughed. He laughed a lot, and I decided I liked that about him even if I wasn't sure whether he was laughing with me or at me.

"How about a soda?" he asked as he pulled into the corner grocery. "Loser's treat."

While he went in to get the soft drinks, I ran my hand over the red cloth seats, telling myself over and over that it was really me, Wendi Collins, in Rod Westmore's car. He not only knew I was alive. He was buying me a soda.

I thought I'd be tongue-tied with the wonder of it all when he came back, but instead I found words spilling out of my mouth without a bit of trouble as we talked about playing volleyball and then drifted over to football.

Rod said, "Your dad must be a football fan."

"Not really," I admitted. "Dad goes fishing sometimes, but mostly he likes to read."

"Read? What's he read?"

"Everything. Don't you like to read?"

"I've never done much of it except what I have to do for school. Football takes a lot of time, and then I make sure I get plenty of sleep so I'll be sharp for the games."

"That sort of cuts into the dating, I guess." Again my words surprised me, as if some other girl were talking inside me and I had nothing at all to do with what she said.

"I date as much as I want to." He looked at me with that smile again.

"I'm sure you do," I said, glad to see my street looming up ahead. "Here's my turn."

Even before he'd pulled the car to a stop in front of my house I was trotting out my manners. "Thanks so much for the ride and the Coke. Maybe next time it'll be my treat."

He caught my arm before I could open the door. "What's your hurry? Are you gong to flit away like one of your famous butterflies?"

"They aren't my butterflies. Butterflies are free."

"Speaking of free," he said. "Are you free next Friday?"

With my heart hammering up in my throat, I managed to pretend a calm I didn't feel. "I thought I'd go to the game."

"Yeah, me too," he said with a twinkle in his blue eyes. "I meant later. I thought maybe you'd like to go to the sock hop with me."

"What about Vanessa?"

His grin slipped down to his mouth to become a sideways smile. "I'm sure Vanessa will be there, but I wasn't asking her. I'm asking you."

As I searched for the right way to say yes, he said, "Gee, kid, I'm not used to begging. Either you want to go or you don't."

"Of course I'd like to go with you," I said quickly. "It's just that sometimes I'm not sure if you're serious or not. I keep thinking maybe you're just egging me on like I'm a big joke or something."

"You're no joke, butterfly girl. A little funny sometimes, but no joke."

I pulled away from his hand and jumped out of the car. "See you Monday," I said lightly before I started up the walk. I wouldn't let myself turn and watch him take off, but I listened till I heard him go around the corner. Only then did I notice Jeff watching me from his driveway.

"Hi, Jeff. How'd you do at the meet?"

When he just stared at me, I went over to him. "What's the matter? Are you sick or something?"

"You might say that," he said finally with that weird crease between his eyes and the little twitch at the corner of his mouth that meant he was upset.

"Did you get hurt at the meet?" I looked down at his ankles for the tape that would mean a running injury.

"No. As a matter of fact, I had my best time ever, and our team won."

"But that's wonderful. I wish I'd been there to take your picture."

"How could you be? You had to be at the park catching bugs. Looks like you didn't have much luck." He pointed at my empty jar. "Catching bugs, that is." He turned away from me and started toward his house.

I grabbed his arm and pulled him around where I could see his face. "What exactly does that mean?"

"It means you've been with Rod Westmore, who's got some reputation with the girls, and you're looking more than a little disheveled. That's what it means."

My eyes popped open wide as I realized exactly what he was thinking. "I can't believe this. We've been at the park catching bugs. A whole bunch of kids were there, and after the bug catching, we played volleyball. I ended up looking a mess like I always do.''

"So Rod, gentleman that he is, gallantly offered to drive you home.''

"Exactly,'' I said tightly. "I don't know how you could think anything else.''

"Let's just say I've seen Rod's magnetism in action.''

"You've got him all wrong. He can't help it if girls keep throwing themselves at him.''

"Poor guy. We should all be so unlucky.'' Jeff turned back toward his house, and this time I let him go.

Still I didn't like for him to be mad at me so I tried one more time. "I almost caught a cricket for you at the park.''

"I can catch my own bugs,'' he said just before he went inside and slammed the door in my face.

Why was everybody getting mad at me? I was the one who should be mad.

The thought didn't help. I still felt bad as I went in to take a shower. Even thinking about going to the sock hop with Rod didn't help too much. What good was it having something special happen to you if there was no one to tell about it?

Chapter 6

On the way downstairs to help Mom put dinner on the table, I practiced the words I'd use to tell her about riding home from the park in Rod's car and how he'd invited me to the sock hop. I thought she would smile and ask me where Rod lived or who his parents were. Or comment on my first date. But when I got to the kitchen, for some reason the words stuck in my throat.

While I set the table I kept hoping she'd say something about me going to the park or ask how the bug collecting was going. I paused in the middle of folding a napkin to slide under the forks. Mom probably didn't even know I was collecting insects.

Finally I just blurted out, "Rod Westmore gave me a lift home from the park today."

Mom looked up from mashing the potatoes. "Is he the one who was here the other night getting his homework?"

"That's the one. The football hero," I added for emphasis. "He's asked me to the sock hop next week."

"That's nice, dear. Maybe I can buy you a new sweater when I go to the city Monday. What color would you like?" Suddenly she raised her head and sniffed the air. "Oh no, I hope I haven't let the rolls burn."

And that was that. I had a date—my first date— with Rod Westmore and all Mom could say was how nice. I'd wanted her to say oh wow and congratulate me on my outstanding achievement. And it was an outstanding achievement for me to get a date with Rod Westmore.

The trouble was I wasn't feeling as excited as I'd expected to feel myself. Maybe it just hadn't had time to sink in that it was actually true, I told myself as I put the rest of the napkins by the plates. And then having Jeff as well as Tracy mad at me made it hard to feel good about anything.

I looked out the window toward Jeff's house, but the door was closed and no one was out in the back- yard. I watched the door a moment, hoping it would open, before I turned abruptly away from the win- dow. Why should I let him ruin my day? A day that had turned out special after all. Later, when I was alone in my room, I'd make a list of reasons why it had been special. Maybe that was the best way to enjoy special things, by yourself alone where you could hold them close inside of you and relive the good parts over and over.

Jason came into the kitchen, grabbed one of the rolls Mom had just taken out, pinched a piece of ham, hugged Mom, and punched me practically all at the same time. When Jason's in a room it seems like the walls draw back a little to give him room. Dad says he has force of personality.

"Hi, Jase," I said with a big smile. "How's school?"

"Do you realize how many times I've been asked

78

that question today?'' Jason said with an exaggerated sigh. ''You'd think everybody in Brookfield had a vested interest in my progress at college.''

''Sorry. I didn't really want to know anyway.''

''That's the way it always is. People ask things they really don't want to know.''

I groaned. ''Not a philosophical treatise, please.''

''The mind should be open to receive new ideas at all times, little sis. In one's kitchen or in a classroom, a person never knows when he might catch the glimmer of a great truth.''

''How long are you staying?'' I asked too sweetly.

''You're getting quicker on the comebacks, sis. In another year or two you might even be fun to talk with.''

''Maybe,'' I said, giving up the fight.

But Jason wasn't through with me yet. Straddling one of the chairs and fixing his eyes on me, he said, ''What's all this nonsense about butterflies?''

I managed to keep from spilling the glass of tea that I was carrying to the table, but only just barely. ''It's nothing that concerns you,'' I said shortly. I wasn't about to get into an argument with Jason about the merits of live butterflies over dead ones.

''Don't you want to get into a good college?''

That caught Mom's attention for the first time, and she looked up from the cabinet at me. I wavered between hoping she'd insist on knowing what was going on and hoping she'd let it pass as I sent Jason a murderous look.

But Maddie took their attention away from me by somersaulting into the kitchen. Literally. All Mom said was ''Remember to hollow out, Madelaine.''

If I had somersaulted into the kitchen when I was

Maddie's age, I'd have been told to go back to my room and try a new approach. But then if I had somersaulted into the kitchen I would have probably knocked over the table and at least three chairs. Actually Maddie hardly ever just walked anywhere. She danced up and down the stairs with her feet arched like a ballet dancer's, and she did back springs with no hands across the living room without rattling the figurines on the shelf.

Now she managed to make everybody forget all about me and butterflies and colleges as she began recounting her accomplishments since she'd last seen Jason. When she ended her recitation, she asked him, "How's school?"

He didn't groan or frown or anything. He just smiled and said, "Great, kid, just great. I tell all my buddies that my little sis is going to be an Olympic champion someday."

I felt like doing a somersault and dumping the table in his lap, but of course I didn't. I sat down like the good plain ordinary girl I'd always been and choked down my food while I listened to them talk. Nobody asked me how my day had been. Nobody noticed that I wasn't hungry. Nobody cared.

After dinner I retreated to my room. The three jars of dead bugs lined up on my desk made me queasy, and I stuck them all out of sight in my closet. Then I sat down with my notebook and began making a list of the reasons it had been a special day. Rod Westmore had asked me to the sock hop. I'd ridden in his car. Mom had baked both a pie and a cake for dessert. That was all I could think of. All the reasons it had been a horrible day kept pushing in from the sides, but I wouldn't write those down.

The next day after lunch, Jason left for school. Since it was a four-hour drive, he didn't expect to get back home before Thanksgiving. "Too much going on up there," he said. And I could imagine the whirl of activities with him in the middle of all of them.

"Just don't forget to study," Dad said.

"Sure, Dad," Jason said pleasantly. "Actually I'm hitting the books more now than I ever did. When you get to college you realize the need for good study habits."

"Sometimes I think you just say what you think people want to hear," I muttered under my breath.

Jason must have heard at least part of what I said because he gave me a funny look and threw me his duffle bag. "Here, Wendi, help me carry my stuff out." He picked up a box of sweaters that had a bag of apples and another chocolate cake Mom must have baked for him early that morning on top.

I helped him stow the stuff in the back of his little car. When I stood up to tell him good-bye, he said, "You never did tell me what was going on with this butterfly nonsense."

"That's because you really didn't want to know," I said, turning his words of the day before on him.

"Mark one up for the kid," he said with a smile. "But whatever this other is about, I'd cut it out if I were you before Scary Mary lowers the boom on you."

"It's all blown up out of proportion. Actually there's not that much to it. I just don't want to kill butterflies for my insect collection, that's all."

"I think maybe you've taken on the wrong teacher, Wendi. Lunsford's different from most. She won't put up with any silliness."

"It's not exactly silly."

"Is that supposed to mean you're not going to back down?"

I met his look. "It means I'm not killing any butterflies."

"You've got guts, kid." He grinned and poked me. "And who knows? Maybe Lunsford won't kill you, but rest assured if she does, I'll send flowers to the funeral."

After Jason left, Maddie went over to play with Kristy, and I went back to my room to begin cataloging the few insects I had caught in the backyard last Saturday. I refused to let my eyes follow Maddie over to Jeff's house or wait while she knocked on the door. Neither would I let my eyes stray to the phone even if I was dying to talk to Tracy.

When I finally escaped from my room and went out into the backyard I told myself it wasn't because I wanted Jeff to see me and come over and apologize. I just needed a break from bugs.

Maddie was sitting on the back stoop rotating her feet and exercising her ankles. She looked as lonely as I felt. "What's wrong, kid? I thought you went over to play with Kristy."

"She wasn't home." Maddie's eyes were full of unshed tears. "She's playing over at Jan's house."

"Oh, I see." I sat down beside her. "Well, why don't you just go over to Jan's? I'll walk with you if you want me to."

Maddie shook her head. "Jan doesn't like me."

"Don't be silly, Maddie. Everybody likes you."

"No, they don't." She looked up at me. "Sometimes you don't like me."

"Of course I always like you, Maddie. You're my

sister," I rushed to say. Her eyes on me were large and round and shining with tears. "All sisters get aggravated at each other every once in a while. I'll bet you're not so fond of me either sometimes."

"I always like you. I wish I was just like you."

"No, you don't," I said firmly. "You're special, Maddie. Really special."

"That's why Jan doesn't like me." Maddie looked down at her feet as she rotated them first one way and then the other. "And now Kristy won't like me anymore either."

"Yes, she will." I wished Mom would show up to help me out with the right words. "It's just that you've been so busy what with your practicing and all. You can't expect Kristy to just sit home and wait till you have a spare minute to play."

"But I'm always home on Sundays."

"Not always. Sometimes you go to the Y and practice," I reminded her gently.

"Only when I have to learn a new trick by Monday."

"I know that, and Kristy knows that too. The trouble is you've got all this special stuff happening to you with your new lessons and Coach Barton and all, but Kristy has things happening to her, too, that while they might not seem quite so exciting as the things happening to you, they're important to her and she needs somebody to share them with."

"Does that mean she won't be my friend anymore?"

"Of course not. It just means that it will be different." My words were doubling back on me until I wasn't sure if I was talking to Maddie or myself.

"I don't want it to be different."

83

"I know, Maddie, but sometimes to do one thing you have to give up something else."

"I know, and I'd rather do gymnastics than anything. But everything's been so hard this week." Maddie leaned over against me. "I can't get enough height on my double somie off the beam and I'm afraid I'm going to hit my head and Coach Barton says I can't be afraid. And Mama's mad because I haven't picked out my music, but I don't know what to pick. And I'm just so tired." Her voice was muffled against me.

I tightened my arms around her. "You'll work it out, kid. What do you say I take some pictures of you doing flips or something."

"I don't feel like doing flips." She looked up with tears streaking down her cheeks. I tried to remember the last time I'd seen her really cry, but I couldn't. "Will you help me, Wendi? You know lots of songs."

I looked out over her head, and there was a butterfly dancing on the wind. Before I could think better of it, I said, 'How about something about butterflies? Tracey said you were light as a butterfly the other day."

The next morning it was raining when I woke up. The weather matched the way I was feeling as I stared into my closet and tried to find something reasonably presentable to wear to school. I finally settled on an old pair of blue jeans I hadn't worn for a year and a red checked shirt because I thought maybe the red would cheer me up. It didn't work.

At least Maddie seemed to have bounced back to her normal confident self. When I went down to the kitchen, she and Mom were discussing every song they could think of that had anything to do with butterflies. I tried not to listen, for though I had given Maddie the butterfly idea freely, I was afraid if I thought about it I'd resent her taking over the only special thing I'd ever had.

Mom drove us to school. After we let Maddie out, she said, "Thanks, Wendi, for helping Madelaine out with her music."

"It was just a thought. You don't have to use it if you don't want to."

"Oh, Madelaine's excited about it. I think this butterfly bit is going to be just the trick to get her past this tough spot she's been having in her work." She glanced over at me with a wide smile and then back at the road. "I hope it quits raining before this afternoon. I hate to make that drive in the rain."

Mom pulled away from the grade school and headed through the morning traffic that piled up on the road leading to Brookfield High. "Good golly," she said. "This is worse than city traffic. I'll be glad when Jeff gets his license so you can ride to school with him."

Jeff, who already had his permit, had been counting the days till he could take his driving test. "He might not want me to ride with him," I said.

Mom gave me a quick, surprised look. "Something wrong between you two?"

"I'm not sure. What's his mom say?"

"I was too busy to talk to her this weekend. Should I have?"

"No, I guess not. Anyway I'm not mad at Jeff."

"But he's mad at you."

"I don't know whether mad is the right word," I said carefully. "He's a little upset because I let Rod bring me home from the park Saturday."

"Why?" Mom's eyes were sharp as she glanced over at me. "Doesn't he like Rod?"

"Rod's okay," I said quickly. "And Jeff always liked him okay before."

"Oh." Mom put a lot of meaning into that little word, and I was glad she was pulling up to the school so she wouldn't have time to spell out exactly what she meant by that oh.

"See you later," I said as I slid out the door. "Maybe it'll stop raining before you have to leave for the city."

Mom looked like she wanted to say more, but she couldn't very well sit there blocking traffic while I stood out in the rain. So she just waved and pulled off. I wondered if she'd go home and call Jeff's mother at work, but then I doubted it. She'd have forgotten all about me and Jeff by the time she got home. She had to worry about finding Maddie's music.

Glancing around warily, I went into the school. Sure enough, there in place of the football poster that had been up Friday was a new butterfly. The poster was a full-color photograph of a pipe-vine swallowtail resting on a white chrysanthemum. The butterfly looked so real I almost expected it to flutter its blue-green wings and fly away if I got too close.

As I stared at it admiring the photographer's talent, I idly thought I should pull it down, but there was no Save the Butterflies slogan printed on it anywhere. It was just a beautiful picture that could only brighten up an otherwise dreary day like a bit of sunshine. I wasn't about to throw sunshine in the trash can.

Of course there were plenty of Save the Butterflies slogans up everywhere else, not to mention a number of Down with Scary Mary's. I pulled down a few of these as I wondered just who was taking the time to make so many signs. Surely they had something better to do. I knew I had something better to do than pull them all down, so I decided to pull Mrs. Lunsford's trick and just pretend I didn't see any of them. If Mr. Browning asked me about them, I'd say, ''What signs?'' Respectfully, of course.

I planned to talk to Tracy at lunch, but when I spotted her in the hall she was with Stewie. They were walking together in front of me with her hand in Stewie's back pocket and his in hers. I couldn't very well disturb intimacy like that.

The rain kept up all day. Even the inside of the school building was dreary in spite of the thousands of lights burning brightly.

I was later than usual getting to biology class and found myself walking in just in front of Rod. Before we went through the door he gave me a little punch and said, ''Hey, kid.''

Smiling back at him, I wished for the first time all day that I hadn't worn my old jeans.

There was a little shuffle as I walked into the room and everybody looked up and stared at me. I almost looked down to see if I'd ripped a seam somewhere. The only person who didn't look up at me was Jeff. He was pretending to be studying intently, but I could see that his book was open to the wrong page.

After Rod reached back, poked my knee, and sort of pointed toward the board, I finally noticed what had gotten the class in such a state of expectation.

There in big letters all across Mrs. Lunsford's blackboard was the slogan I had made famous at Brookfield High: Save the Butterflies. Below it in slightly smaller letters was ''Scary Mary doesn't scare us." My mouth fell open as I stared at it and wondered who could have possibly had the nerve to actually brave the lion's den long enough to stand there in plain sight and scribble out that message. I looked down at the floor, half expecting to see some poor soul's wasted body lying there.

All at once I noticed other eyes sliding over to look at me, and I was further astounded to realize they thought I had written the message there, crediting me with far more courage than I had. Then, as my eyes swung up to where Mrs. Lunsford sat calmly at her desk waiting for the bell to ring as if nothing out of the ordinary were happening, I knew I'd better find some courage somewhere because round two was just about to begin.

As soon as the bell rang, Mrs. Lunsford's voice took command of the room. "Miss Collins, erase the board," she said without looking up.

With my heart pounding, I walked to the board. There wasn't a sound in the room, and the scratch of the eraser as it buffed the board was extra loud. Turning to go back to my seat, I wondered why in the world I'd been dumb enough to wear this red shirt. My face had to be red enough to match.

Mrs. Lunsford didn't look up until I was back in my seat. Then she began the lesson just like any other day without even glancing my way. In fact she seemed to make an extra effort to be pleasant. The last twenty minutes of class she let us use her books to find the scientific names of the insects we'd captured over the weekend, allowing a certain low-volume whispering as the students compared pictures of insects.

It wasn't until the bell rang that she said, "Miss Collins, stay after class."

I'd been expecting it the whole hour, but the words still pierced through me and made my heart go to hammering again. Jeff smiled at me for the first time in what seemed like weeks. I felt better than I had all day in spite of the fact I was about to go another round with Scary Mary.

She gave me the quiet treatment again as the last kid filed out of the room with a backward curious glance. This time she waited three whole minutes and I was about to say something just because I couldn't stand the silence another second when she looked up.

"Sit down, Wendi."

I sat down in the chair she motioned to next to her desk, my apprehension growing because she'd used my first name for the first time all year.

"I gather you've had plenty of time to think over what we talked about last time I asked you to stay after class."

"Yes, ma'am."

"And you decided to keep on with this silly charade." The first timbre of crossness slipped into her voice, and hearing it, she cleared her throat.

"Not exactly, ma'am," I said cautiously.

She actually smiled at me. "What then? Exactly."

"I took down all my posters and signs just like Mr. Browning told me to. I don't want to break any of the school's rules."

"And then you put them all back up again."

"No, ma'am, I didn't put any more up."

She leaned back in her chair and stared at me. "I want to believe you. Still, signs and posters don't regenerate themselves. Someone is putting them up. Someone wrote that . . ." She paused as though searching for the proper words to describe the desecration of her blackboard. Finally she cleared her throat again and went on. "Those words on my board. What is your explanation for that?"

"I don't know how that got there, Mrs. Lunsford." I looked straight at her though my insides were quaking and added, "I certainly wouldn't have had the courage to put it there."

She laughed, and the sound was so surprising I couldn't quite keep from jumping. Mrs. Lunsford noticed, and the amused look stayed on her face even after the laugh died away. "You didn't think I knew how to laugh, did you?"

I searched my mind for the proper response. If I said yes, of course I knew she could laugh, I'd be lying since I hadn't been at all sure she ever laughed. Still I couldn't very well say no, ma'am, I didn't think you could laugh. I ended up sort of half nodding and half shaking my head.

"Well, Miss Wendi Collins," she said, putting her hands together in front of her face and tapping her long forefingers together. "It looks like we both have a problem."

"Yes, ma'am."

"Do you know how many years I've been teaching biology?"

"Fifteen?"

She smiled a little wryly. "What happened to your sense of honesty there, Miss Collins? Maybe I should rethink whether to believe you about the signs."

"Twenty-three years."

"In fact it's been twenty-four. I've taught biology to some of the most reluctant students you're ever likely to see in a classroom. I've pushed and pounded and even rammed facts into their tightly closed minds, but they knew something about biology when they left my class." She leaned forward toward me. "Do you like biology?"

"No."

"Neither did I when I was in high school. I planned to be a home economics teacher."

"Home ec? You mean family living?"

Again she looked amused. "The thought sort of surprises me, too, when I think about it now. But I like teaching biology. It's an important subject and one that most high school students are embarrassingly ignorant of."

"Yes, ma'am," I said because she paused as if she expected me to say something.

"Do you think I'm a good teacher?" She held up her hand before I could answer. "Note I didn't ask if I was a likable teacher. What I asked was whether you think I am competent at relaying information to you, a student."

"I expect to learn a lot about biology this year."

"Because you want to?" She lifted her eyebrows as she spoke.

"Because you'll insist that I learn as much as I can."

She smiled a little and sat back. "Now then, Miss Collins, what are you going to do about this butterfly craze you've started?"

"I don't know."

"I want it stopped."

"I'm not sure I can. I mean every time I take down the posters, more posters appear almost like magic. The whole thing seems to have taken on a life of its own."

"Magic has nothing to do with it," Mrs. Lunsford

said, frowning for the first time. "And even if your motives are pure in all this, I'm not sure that goes for all your cohorts."

I thought of the Scary Mary posters and slogans and felt uncomfortable.

She went on. "So you see I must take a firm line. Rules are rules in my class. They aren't broken or even bent without some sort of punishment doled out."

"Yes, ma'am. I'm prepared for that."

She stared at me for a long moment before she looked down at the papers on her desk and said, "Very well. You're dismissed."

Chapter 7

I was relieved to see the hallway empty when I left the room. I didn't like the idea of people waiting around to see what I'd look like after Mrs. Lunsford got through with me.

I took a deep breath and was surprised to realize I wasn't trembling even a little bit. The fact was the more I had talked to Mrs. Lunsford the less afraid of her I was and the worse I felt for causing her so much trouble.

I had no idea that my wild and crazy butterfly campaign was going to snowball into some sort of student revolt against her. Any other teacher might have laughed it off, and the kids would have just dropped the whole thing as boring. Mrs. Lunsford couldn't do that. Discipline was too important to her, and if some student had to be sacrificed in order for her to maintain her reputation as a teacher who countenanced absolutely no nonsense, then that student would be sacrificed.

As I shifted my books, my eyes caught on a "Take a Stand Against Scary Mary. Stop Cruelty to Butterflies" sign. I yanked it down, ripped it apart, and stuck it in the trash.

I stopped on the stairs going toward the doors,

watching the rain bounce off the sidewalk outside. "Perfect," I muttered.

"What's perfect?" Rod asked behind me.

I looked around at him. "Where did you come from?"

He arched his eyebrows and grinned at me. "You aren't that young and innocent, are you? Maybe I'm the one who should tutor you in biology."

He was trying to fluster me, and I was tired of being flustered for one day. I didn't even blush as I said calmly, "I meant I didn't see you in the hall."

"I was waiting up here for you."

Rod Westmore was waiting for me. The thought skipped happily through my mind. "What about football practice?"

"The coach let us off today since the field would be a loblolly."

"I thought you always had to lift weights."

"We never won two games in a row before. He's rewarding us. Of course he'll probably just work us twice as hard tomorrow to make up for it. Anyway I was just hanging around to see if you wanted a ride home."

We walked out front together where I spotted Jeff's mother's car parked across the drive. She must have taken off work to pick up Kristy and Jeff. I turned to Rod and said, "Thanks, but there's my neighbor waiting for me."

"Are you sure? Looks like to me they're leaving."

When I turned back around, sure enough, the car was pulling away. I waved at them, but they didn't stop.

"Guess you're stuck with me, unless you'd rather walk in the rain," Rod said.

I started to, just to make them feel bad when I got home, but I'm not quite that stupid. Besides, any girl would jump at the chance to ride with Rod Westmore.

We ran through the rain to his car in the parking lot. After we were inside he looked at me and laughed. "You're wet."

I sighed, knowing the rain would have knocked out what little curl my hair had and that it would be drooping down around my face. My shirt had lost all its crispness and hung on me like a limp rag. "I must look a mess," I said.

"Sort of. That's one good thing about getting your hair clipped off short for football." With a grin, he shook his head. "You just shake like a dog, and you're ready to go again."

"You always look great," I said matter-of-factly. "Some kids do, you know, and then there are the others like me who never look great."

"I don't know about that."

He made no move to start the car, and as the windows began to fog up, the rain pounding down on the car roof seemed to be isolating us from the rest of the world. I began to feel a little nervous even before he brushed some raindrops off my cheek with the back of his hand.

"Tell me, butterfly girl," he said with that amused glint in his eye. "What do butterflies do in the rain?"

"I don't know. Maybe they hide under a big leaf."

"Do you suppose the boys and girls hide together? Is that where all the little caterpillars come from?"

"Could be," I said casually. "I'd better get home. Mom might be worried." It wasn't exactly a lie. Mom might have been worried if she'd been at home.

"What's the matter, little butterfly? You afraid to land in any one spot with me for long?"

"I don't want to make any little caterpillars."

He laughed and started up the car. As he let the defroster run to clear the windshield, he said, "What did the old bat do to you?"

It was a minute before I realized he was talking about Mrs. Lunsford. "Oh, she's not so bad," I said.

"You're really funny sometimes, butterfly girl. Scary Mary not so bad? That's like saying a broken neck's not so bad."

"No, really. I mean it. And I feel sort of bad the way everything's gotten a little out of hand with the butterflies and everything."

"You about to go out and catch butterflies?" He glanced over at me with a little grin. "You can't disturb them now. They're busy under their leaves."

I ignored his last comment. "I'm not putting any butterflies in my collection, but I wouldn't blame the other kids if they did. Nobody wants a bad grade."

"I'm happy as long as I get good enough grades to stay out of trouble with the coach."

"But you need good grades to get into college."

"A football player doesn't need anything but ability to get into college."

"Most kids aren't lucky enough to have that kind of special talent. Most of us are just average."

"Yeah, that makes it a lot easier for the rest of us who aren't."

"You mean to get into college?" I asked.

"That and other things," he said with another look over at me.

I was glad to see my house through the rain. I pushed open the door before he pulled completely to a stop and was halfway out in the rain when he said, "Some of us will be over later. We thought we might work ahead on our biology."

"Well sure, I guess that'll be okay," I said while I tried to remember if Dad was going to be home. The half of me that was out of the car was getting soaked.

"I think mostly the kids want to see if you survived your bout with Mrs. Lunsford."

"Really, she's not that bad."

It was a line I had to repeat a dozen times before the night was over. Even Tracy, when she showed up with Stewie, had gotten over her spat with me enough to want to know what had happened with Mrs. Lunsford.

Tracy hooted when I repeated my line in defense of Mrs. Lunsford. "Not so bad, eh? She had you quivering in your socks last week."

I gave it up and let them think what they wanted. After all, I doubted if Mrs. Lunsford wanted the kids to think she was nice. She just wanted us to learn biology and to know she wouldn't put up with any nonsense.

Before Tracy went back to sit by Stewie, I said, "Look, I'm sorry about Saturday."

Tracy looked relieved that I'd brought it up. "Me too, Wendi. We must have been affected by the heat."

"Or something." We both giggled because we knew I meant boys.

"And I guess I was wrong to say what I did. I mean it looks like you snagged Rod in spite of spiking that ball at him."

"Or maybe because of it."

"I heard he was taking you to the sock hop. Is that true?" Tracy asked.

"How did you know? I haven't told anybody except Mom."

"Rod must have told Vanessa."

"I guess that's why she didn't show up tonight to simper all over him."

"I guess. Anyway Vanessa's going around telling everybody it must be some kind of joke." Tracy mocked Vanessa as she added, "I mean how in the world could any sane male in his right mind pick anybody over her?"

"I've been wondering about that, too," I said with an attempt at a smile.

"Is something wrong, Wendi? It's not really a joke, is it?"

"I don't know. What do you think?"

"Quit putting yourself down, Wendi. You're cute and lots more fun to talk to than Vanessa. I talked to her today at lunch and she really is pretty empty-headed. Maybe Rod was just tired of girls who simper all over him, and he liked the way you didn't run after him."

"Didn't run after him? If you will recall that's what made you think up this whole mess with the butter-flies to begin with."

"And it worked like a dream. For both of us." She glanced over to where Stewie was talking to some of the boys. Then she seemed to remember what we were talking about and said, "But you sort of tried to back away once Rod did notice you."

"You think so?"

"I know so. It scared you that Rod had actually noticed you. Before it had all been in your imagination, but this was the real boy you were going to have to talk to. Have you let him kiss you yet?"

I stepped back from Tracy. "For heaven's sake, I've only talked to him a few times."

Tracy smiled her superior know-it-all smile. "See, what did I tell you?"

"I don't see any need to rush things." I looked at her curiously before I asked, "Have you and Stewie— Stewart I mean—well, have you, you know?"

Tracey sighed a little as if she were about to float off the floor. "Stewart has very expressive lips." A dreamy look flooded her eyes as she pushed her hair back from her face.

I wanted to ask her if Stewie took off his glasses first, but I was afraid she'd get mad at me again. So I just smiled and felt a little silly and more than a little disappointed. I'd never thought Tracy would discover the special thrill of kissing before I did. Of course I could have kissed Rod that afternoon in the parking lot at school. All I'd had to have done was lean toward his hand when he brushed my cheek.

It surprised me that I realized that. Maybe some things about boys came instinctively to all girls. But would kissing? I wasn't sure I'd know how to do it right with a boy like Rod Westmore who had probably kissed dozens of girls. Funny thing was, I had the feeling that if I was worried about how to kiss somebody then I didn't really want to bad enough. Kissing ought to be something that just happened during a moment of closeness. Not something to practice ahead of time. Or should it?

Rod was the last to leave. He caught my hand before he went out the door and gave it a little squeeze. "Don't forget about Friday night."

"I won't," I said, and I tried to feel special. I honestly did. But instead of special, I just kept feeling worried. Worried that I'd do something wrong to make him laugh. Worried that it was all just a joke. Worried that I was going to get an F in biology and worried that Jeff and I would never really be close friends again. Worried that everyone around me was changing and I'd be left behind.

That night as I lay in bed listening to the rain spatter up against my window, I remembered what I'd told Maddie the day before. People changed and so did friendships. But I resisted my words the same as Maddie had. Like her, I wanted it all. I could see no reason why Rod giving me a ride home from the park had to make Jeff quit talking to me any more than Maddie could understand why her hectic practice schedule had to affect her friendship with Kristy.

Of course it wasn't exactly the same. Maddie was growing away from Kristy, growing away from all of us in a way. She didn't really have any choice. She had to make sacrifices to her talent, but I wasn't growing away from anybody.

Even though my butterfly campaign had given me a bit of notoriety, I was still the same ordinary girl I'd always been, with nothing special to speak of except my crazy love for butterflies, and I'd even given that away to Maddie. They weren't mine and mine alone anymore. When I thought about it, I supposed they never had been mine. Butterflies can't actually belong to anybody. But I'd wanted them to be mine.

I sat up in bed and looked out my window toward Jeff's house. His window was right across from mine, and when we were kids we used to talk to each other at night over walkie-talkies. I wondered now if he missed talking to me as much as I missed talking to him.

I settled back down on my pillow, but it was a long time before I could go to sleep. And then I dreamed about butterflies dancing with Maddie.

By the middle of the week, the butterfly craze was settling to a simmer at school. I was glad, since I was tired of tearing down posters and scraping stickers off the wall, so tired that I left the pictures of butterflies alone and only went after the Scary Mary posters.

Even Mrs. Lunsford seemed to be willing to let the whole mess ride as long as no one else desecrated her blackboard. There were only a few more days for insect collecting. Monday was the turn-in day, and everybody was too busy in class trying to identify the insects they already had to worry too much about all the butterflies still fluttering around outside. My bugs were still in their jars in the back of my closet.

Rod and I didn't get much chance to talk during the day and football practice took most of his free time as the coach anxiously geared up for his third win. The one time Rod called me, we ran out of anything to say after he told me about football practice and I told him about the funny green and orange spotted bug I'd seen on the way home. There'd been an awkward silence while I tried desperately to think of something witty to say. Finally he said he'd see me Friday night and hung up. He kept reminding me about the sock hop. As if any girl could forget a date with Rod Westmore.

On Thursday I still hadn't gotten an opportunity to talk to Jeff. It wasn't that I hadn't tried. On Tuesday I had practically followed him around begging him for a chance to talk, but he'd brushed me off as though I were selling vacuum cleaners. My pride hurt, I resolved to give him the same silent treatment he was giving me.

I was proud for almost two days, but by Thursday afternoon I felt so bad I had to give it one more try. I was glad my camera gave me an excuse to go out to the cross-country meet. He'd have to talk to me there.

The first person I saw when I got out to the course was Vanessa, who as far as I knew had never been to a cross-country meet in her entire life. I thought she'd shoot darts at me with her eyes when she saw me, but instead she came running over to meet me.

"Wendi, I didn't expect you to come to the cross-country meet today."

"I have to take pictures." I held up my camera. "But I don't believe I've ever seen you out here before."

"Oh, but I come to them now."

Something about her voice made me look at her closer. Her eyes were sparkling, and her smile was so big it was almost a giggle. She was fairly popping with some bit of news. "That's great. The cross-country team could use a little support from the cheerleaders."

"I just came out to support one of them," she said.

My mind ran rapidly through all the boys on the team. If there was one who would attract Vanessa's attention, I couldn't recall him. She really was more the football-player type. Like me, I thought with a crooked little smile. I decided to pretend I didn't hear her last remark since I didn't want to get into a guessing game with Vanessa. The fact was she could have any boy in school just by crooking her little finger at him. Any boy but Rod Westmore, that is. So I just asked, "Have they started yet?"

"Yes. You're late." She looked over toward the course. "Jeff was in the lead. He'll probably stay in the lead all the way."

As soon as she said Jeff's name, my stomach sank around about my knees. "So Jeff's the one you came out to support. Since when?"

"I've always thought Jeffie was cute."

"Jeffie?" I wanted to throw up.

"He said I could call him that. Isn't it just the cutest?"

"Oh, simply."

"I suppose he told you he asked me to go to the sock hop. I know you two have been friends since you were in diapers."

"Did he tell you that?"

She shrugged, with a little shake of her beautiful head. "Actually he hasn't said a thing about you. We've been too busy talking about ourselves."

"I'm sure," I said. "So he asked you to the sock hop. Are you meeting him there, or is his mother picking you up? Jeff's only got his permit, you know."

She laughed, releasing beautiful tinkling tones from her mouth into the clear fall sunshine. "You mean he hasn't told you."

"Hasn't told me what?"

"He got his license yesterday," she said with a bright, victorious smile.

"That's wonderful," I forced myself to say before I turned to leave. I could see the runners in the distance, and I didn't want to be anywhere near this place when the race ended.

"Aren't you going to take pictures of the finish?" Vanessa said.

With effort I called back cheerfully, "No, I just remembered I forgot to bring film. I'll catch them next meet."

"I'll congratulate Jeffie for you when he wins. I'll give him two kisses. One for me and one for you."

It was a long walk home from the course, and with every step my hurt feelings swelled larger. Jeff and I had been looking forward to getting our driver's licenses for years. Before he took his test for his permit, I'd helped him study his road manual until we both knew it frontwards and backwards. He'd promised to take me down to the Burger Place for a milk shake the very day he got his license. Now not only had he not kept that promise, he hadn't even told me about it. I'd had to hear the news from Vanessa. Vanessa, of all people.

When I got home I went straight to the phone and called Tracy, but Tracy's mother told me she was at Stewart's house studying math. Or something, I thought sourly, but I kept my mouth shut.

I stashed my books on the steps and went into the kitchen to start supper for me and Dad. Mom's note was propped up in the middle of the table like always, but I crumpled it up and threw it away without reading it. I'd fix whatever I wanted to for supper, and I already knew about the load of washing that needed doing and the floors that needed sweeping and the dishes that needed washing. Didn't I do the same things every afternoon?

I stared around the kitchen, sick and tired of being good, dependable Wendi. All I wanted to do was go to my room, shut the door, and pull the covers up over my head. I didn't even feel like making a list of the reasons why it was all right for me to cry. But there wasn't anybody else to do the chores, and I didn't know what excuse I could give Mom when she dragged in late tonight so tired she could hardly smile, much less worry about my problems.

Besides, what would I tell her were my problems? So Jeff hadn't told me he'd gotten his driver's license. That was hardly something to feel like dying over. And so Tracy was busy with Stewie. Did I expect her to sit at home by the phone just waiting for me to have a little problem to talk out with her? I mean what kind of problems could I have? I had a date with Rod Westmore.

I was glad I was cutting up an onion for our hamburgers when Dad came in. That explained the tears.

Chapter 8

I felt so awful when I woke up Friday morning I was tempted to just stay in bed. But Mom would have wanted to know my symptoms, and there wasn't anything specific I could say was hurting like a sore throat or a headache. Besides, even if I had a raging fever I would have had to go to school. This was the big day. The day I, ordinary Wendi Collins, had my first, real, actual date with Rod Westmore.

I kept telling myself that as I fixed my hair and put on my makeup. I even practiced a few smiles and one kiss in the mirror, but kissing a mirror leaves a lot to be desired, like a boy and romance. I pulled on my shirt that was supposed to make my eyes blue. My eyes didn't seem to notice as they stayed stubbornly somewhere between green and gray.

Vanessa didn't have to worry about what she wore to make her eyes look blue. They were always blue, a sparkling, clear-sky blue. She must have been watching for me because she pounced out at me as soon as I got to school.

"Oh, hi there, Wendi," she said casually, as though she hadn't fought through three groups of kids to get over to where I was working the combination of my locker.

I muttered as civil a good morning as I could manage, which this morning was little more than a growl.

"You look horrid, Wendi," she said with a delighted smile. "Didn't you sleep well?"

"I think I'm catching a cold." I breathed toward her just in case I really was sick.

"That's too bad. What about your big date tonight?"

"What about it?" I gathered up my books and banged my locker shut with a satisfyingly loud slam.

"Oh, but it would be a shame if you missed your big date with Rod. You know he doesn't go out with just anyone."

"Have you ever gone out with him?" I asked, suddenly interested.

"Of course. Lots of times."

"When?"

"What do you care?" she said, her smile disappearing. "Maybe I should give you a bit of advice. Rod's cute, but he does like to have his way. What he wants, he gets."

"I thought that was the way you were."

She actually smiled again. "I am. That's why I'm going with Jeffie."

"I heard Rod was your first choice."

"People will tell you anything," she said with a light laugh.

"Did Jeff win last night?" I asked when I couldn't think of anything else mean to say.

"Why, didn't he tell you? He set a new school record."

"That's great." I wished now I'd stayed to take pictures even if it would have meant watching Vanessa plant victory kisses on Jeff.

"I thought you and Jeffie were such good friends he told you everything."

"I've been very busy."

"Busy with Rod?" she asked with lifted eyebrows.

"Just busy." I hurried away toward my homeroom. The day went quickly, which was good because I didn't get to feeling any better in spite of the way Rod punched my shoulder and winked at me once when we passed each other in the hall. By biology class I was beginning to wonder if I really was coming down with some kind of bug, the germy kind.

Before class ended, Mrs. Lunsford reminded us that our insect collections would be due Monday. Then she stared at me for a long moment before she let her eyes slide over the rest of the class. "Your collections must contain some species of the order Lepidoptera, which includes Frenatae and Rhopalocera." Just in case there were still some of us who didn't know after two intense weeks of study, she added, "Butterflies and moths."

Again she looked at me. I had the feeling the rest of the class was also trying to look at me without turning their heads. The tension was about to snap audibly in the room when the bell rang and she dismissed us. I kept waiting for her to tell me to stay, but she went on working quietly at her desk as the students began to file out. When I passed her desk, I dared to look over at her, and she glanced up and half smiled.

Rod was waiting outside the door for me. "See you after the game, butterfly girl. I'd offer you a ride home, but the coach would kill me if he saw me so much as talking to a girl before a game." He looked over his shoulder as if he expected the coach to come out of one of the lockers behind him.

"Why?" I asked.

"He thinks girls take our minds off the game."

"I can't believe girls bother your game."

"They never have before." Rod grinned at me.

I wasn't sure what to say to that so I just grinned back.

"Wear your brightest colors, and we'll pretend we're butterflies tonight." He stared into my eyes a minute before he added, "Maybe it'll rain."

I blushed, and he laughed a little as he punched my arm lightly and then loped off up the hall. I followed slowly, almost glad when he was out of sight around the corner. Just what would a boy like Rod Westmore expect from a girl on her first date? I sighed and decided I'd better go home and practice kissing my mirror some more.

I was almost down to the sidewalk in front of the school when Jeff passed in his car. Vanessa was scooted over close to him, and she leaned around Jeff to wave out his window at me. Jeff looked around and waved, too. Somehow, in spite of the funny aching pounding inside my chest, I smiled and waved back.

After they passed on by, I could hardly find the energy to keep walking, and if I hadn't been afraid I'd look so silly, I would have sat down right there in the middle of the sidewalk and rested.

"Hey, how about that Jeff?" Tracy said behind me. She was a little out of breath from rushing to catch up with me. "Who'd have ever thought he'd snag Vanessa?"

I changed the subject without answering her. "Where's Stewie?"

"He had some extra stuff to do after school. I told him I'd walk home. I want to have plenty of time to get ready before he picks me up tonight. Is Rod picking you up?"

"He can't. The coach won't let them think about girls before a game."

"Boys always think about girls," Tracy said. "Do you want me and Stewart to come by for you?"

"You are making a joke. I'm sure Stewart would love to have me dragging along on your date."

"He wouldn't mind. At least not before the game." She gave me a conspiratorial grin. "Now afterwards might be a different matter."

I laughed even though I wasn't sure what I was laughing about and said, "Dad will drive me over."

"Well, okay, but you'll sit with us at the game."

"Sure, why not?"

"You don't look too happy."

"Just nerves, I guess. I've never been out with a boy like Rod Westmore before."

"You've never been out with any boy before," Tracy reminded me.

"You know what I mean."

"Rod's like any other boy. All you've got to do is let him know you think he's great and that you're having a wonderful time."

"When did you get so all-wise?"

"Since Stewart started tutoring me," she said with a happy little laugh. Tracy was so happy lately that sometimes she made me sick.

That night I spent a full two hours getting ready. I'd decided on what I was going to wear days ago when Mom brought me a beautiful new sweater home from the city. It was a deep turquoise blue guaranteed to make my eyes turn their best color. But while the sweater was perfect, everything else was a disaster. I didn't even have any clean socks without holes in them, and I couldn't very well wear socks with holes to a sock hop. I ended up stealing a pair of socks from Mom's drawer.

When I was dressed at last, I looked myself over in the full-length mirror and wished Mom were there to tell me if my pants looked all right with this sweater. I needed Mom's opinion, but she was still in the city with Maddie. Dad, of course, would say I looked nice, but Dad said that when I had on my worst pair of jeans and a ragged sweatshirt.

I considered for a moment going over and asking Jeff's mom what she thought, but only for a moment. It had been a week since Jeff had said anything to me besides a stiff hi when we passed in the hall. Even looking at his house made that ache pound up inside me now, and if I saw Bev I might just cry on her shoulder. I couldn't do that. Tonight was my special night. Certainly not a time for tears.

As I turned to go downstairs, my eye fell on my camera. I grabbed it up. The shots I'd taken of the crowd a couple of weeks ago had turned out great, and besides, Walter couldn't be everywhere. Maybe I could get a shot he'd miss.

When I got to the field, the game had already started, and the stands were just about full. I took a quick look at the scoreboard, but it was all zeros. Then I started searching the crowd for Tracy and Stewie.

I saw Jeff first. He was sitting down toward the

111

bottom of the bleachers right in front of the cheer-leaders. Out on the field Vanessa's tan legs flashed as she kicked and jumped and worked the crowd for enthusiasm.

She was our best cheerleader. Concentrating, I watched her through my viewfinder and waited for the perfect moment. Then I snapped what I knew would be a couple of fantastic shots.

That funny ache sprang up and spread in my chest again as I dropped my camera down away from my eye. All at once I remembered Maddie not wanting to share Kristy with any other friends, and I thought the same thing must be true with me. I didn't want to share Jeff either. But that was silly, I told myself sternly.

Before I had time to think about it, I went over and squeezed in beside him. "Hey, Jeff, I heard about you breaking the school record the other day. That's great," I said. It felt funny to be so nervous talking to him. My heart was actually jumping up inside me.

He turned toward me, and for a minute I was afraid he was going to give me the cold shoulder. His green eyes were so dark and serious. But then he smiled, and I felt a little better.

"I wish I'd been there," I added.

"You were." When I started to shake my head, he went on. "I saw you leaving."

I shrugged a little. "I didn't know you were going to break the record, and I had a lot of homework."

His smile disappeared. "Yeah, I've been busy, too."

"So I've noticed." I looked back out at Vanessa. "She really is gorgeous, but I thought you told me once she wasn't your type."

"I decided I wasn't being open-minded enough about my types." He fixed his eyes on Vanessa again. "Besides, no guy in his right mind would turn down Vanessa."

"Well, you're certainly in your right mind, and you're looking pretty gorgeous yourself tonight." He was wearing a dark green sweater that must have been as new as the one I had on. I wondered vaguely when he had sprouted such broad shoulders. Standing up quickly, I said, "Have you seen Tracy?"

"She and Stewie are over in the next section, I think. You never know who will make a couple, do you?" He looked from the field to me again. "I guess your butterfly scheme worked pretty good for the both of you."

"All it's going to do is get me a bad grade in biology."

"It got you a date with Rod. That's what you wanted, wasn't it?"

He didn't sound anything like the Jeff I knew, and I wanted to shake him and bring back my friend Jeff. But just then the crowd jumped and began roaring over some great play out on the field. I slipped away to find Tracy and Stewie before the roar died away.

The Brookfield Tigers won another game. We were down by a field goal at the start of the fourth quarter, but then we got the ball and began pushing it down the field toward the goal line. Everybody in the stands stayed on their feet. Finally the quarterback snapped the ball and pitched out a little sideways pass to Rod. Allen and another blocker pushed aside the defenders, and then there was nothing between Rod and the goalposts except the grass. As the crowd went wild, Rod rode the cheers all the way across the goal line.

People all around me were banging me on the back and congratulating me as if I'd just made the run down the field. I tried to enjoy being the center of attention and feel special even though it wasn't me they thought was special. It was my date with Rod.

Over the heads I watched Rod dance a little jig as some of the guys slapped him on the back. I climbed down off the bleachers and began taking pictures both of the crowd and the team members on the sidelines who kept celebrating even though play was still in progress out on the field. A few minutes later, after the kick for the extra point went wide, the game was over, and the Brookfield Tigers had won three in a row.

I turned my camera on the cheerleaders streaming out to congratulate the players as they trotted off the field toward the locker room. It didn't even bother me when Vanessa hung herself around Rod's neck. Or when Rod looked down at her and said something with a little laugh. I just thought about the great picture I was getting of them. Then she laughed, too, turned loose of Rod, and grabbed another player.

I glanced over to where Jeff had been sitting to see if he had noticed, but I couldn't find him in the mill of people beginning to move off the bleachers. He was probably somewhere to the side of the field waiting for Vanessa to get all the players hugged so she could start on him. I was glad I couldn't see him, because I didn't want to take a picture of that.

Even though some of the other girls who were going to the sock hop with football players stood around outside the dressing room and waited for them to change, I went on to the dance with Stewie and Tracy.

The sock hop turned into a victory celebration, and

each time a football player entered, the kids let out a big cheer. The biggest cheer went up when Rod pushed through the doors. He held up three fingers, and the kids went wild. I was cheering too. Partly because we had won, but mostly because I'd finally have a date and could stop feeling like the odd man out.

Stewie and Tracy were being nice, but there's not much way three people can dance together. I'd spent most of my time watching Vanessa and Jeff. After she'd pulled him past me for the tenth time, I'd grabbed my camera and started zooming in on the other couples dancing past me.

Now I left my camera on the table and pushed through the kids over to Rod. His hair was still wet from his shower, and a couple of drops of water glistened on his forehead. In jeans and a blue sweater that matched his eyes, he looked great, like always.

"Hey, butterfly girl," he said with a grin. "I thought maybe you'd flown on home and stood me up."

"I wouldn't do that. I just decided to wait for you here. You didn't mind, did you?"

"I guess not. Except all the other guys got victory kisses as soon as they came out of the locker room. I'm one behind."

I couldn't keep from blushing, and he laughed as he grabbed my wrists. "Don't worry, kid. We'll make up for it later. First we'll dance."

Since Rod was a great dancer, I felt a little awkward in comparison, but he never let on that I was anything but the best. We danced fast numbers and slow ones. On the slow ones he held me so close our bodies touched.

"Funny," he whispered in my ear. "You don't feel a bit like a butterfly."

"It's a good thing. You would have crushed my wings by now."

He loosened his hold. "Don't you like the way I feel, little butterfly girl?"

I stumbled around in my mind searching for a cute answer, but I came up empty.

He looked straight into my eyes and said, "I like the way you feel."

I was almost grateful Vanessa picked that moment to bump into us. She had changed out of her cheerleading outfit into a fluffy pink sweater and a short little white skirt that gave full exposure to her gorgeous legs.

"Oh hi, Rod," she said with a big smile at him and a bare glance at me. "Are you having fun?"

"Sure, Essie. How are you and old Jeff here getting along?"

I had to make myself look at Jeff, not sure I could stand to see the bliss that was bound to be radiating from his face after an hour or so of being pressed close to Vanessa on a crowded dance floor. But if there was bliss in his eyes as he looked at me, I couldn't see it. Instead he looked a little uncomfortable and maybe a little tired, like he might have gotten up that morning feeling as awful as I had.

Jeff stared at me for a moment, and I wondered what he was seeing. Was bliss flowing out of my pores? Everybody in the gym seemed to think it should be as they slapped Rod on the back and winked at me as if I were the luckiest girl in the world. And I guess I was. I'd gotten my heart's desire, a date with Rod Westmore, and from the way the kids acted, I'd also been awarded an instant ticket to popularity. Being Rod's date made me special.

"We're getting along fine," Jeff said, his eyes still on me. Then he looked at Rod. "That was a great run."

"From what I've been hearing we could have used you on the team, too. The way you can run we might have buried everybody," Rod said.

Jeff smiled. "Football's not for me. I like running as long as I don't have to worry about being tackled."

"You're not afraid of a little contact, are you, Jeffie?" Vanessa snuggled closer to him.

Rod laughed and said, "I'm sure he's not afraid of that kind of contact, Essie."

I felt a blush blooming up in my cheeks and wondered if I could make some excuse to go to the rest room. If this went on much longer, I wouldn't need to make up an excuse. I'd be sick.

Jeff put his arm around Vanessa. "No, I'm not afraid of contact sports. It's just that I plan to be running for a long time after I graduate, and I've heard of too many guys who have bad knees from playing football. As a runner I can't take that chance."

"To each his own," Rod said.

Jeff just smiled as he began dancing with Vanessa again. As they moved away, Vanessa said, "You all have a good time."

"We plan to, don't we, Miss Butterfly? Especially if we can get it to start raining."

Jeff glanced back over his shoulder at me, but I quickly turned my head so he couldn't see the way my cheeks were flaming.

Rod laughed. "You color up the easiest of any girl I ever knew."

I sighed. "I know, but there just doesn't seem to be any way to stop a blush once it starts. It's embarrassing to blush so easily, and then that makes you blush even more."

"Until you look like a Christmas tree."

"Do I look that bad?" I took my hand away from his neck and pushed it across my cheek as though I could wipe away the red warming my face.

"Who ever said a Christmas tree looked bad? I think it's kind of cute."

I let him pull me a little closer then as I laid my head on his shoulder. I had so many crazy mixed-up feelings zapping through me that I needed a little time without having to talk to think through them.

Besides, if I looked around I might have to see Vanessa and Jeff again.

The sock hop was still going strong when Rod said we'd have to leave. "The coach didn't lift our curfew," he explained. "He gave us the devil after the game."

"But you won."

"Yeah, but not soon enough to suit him. These close ones are hard on his nerves. Anyway he let us know that this night wasn't any different than any other night and that we'd better be home on time."

"How would he know if you weren't?"

"Coach has his ways. You don't mind leaving a little early, do you?"

"Not at all." And I didn't. I was tired of the crowded dance floor and the music, and I was especially tired of everybody suddenly liking me because I was with Rod.

When we went out in the hall, Tracy came over to say good-bye or maybe just to be in on the triumphant finale of her inspiration because she smiled and said, "You two looked great out there on the floor together."

"Hello there, Wendi's friend," Rod said with his slow smile.

Tracy bristled. "My name is Tracy."

"Okay then, hello there, Tracy," Rod said, his smile wider.

Tracy smiled back at him as though she'd won some sort of minor victory, but then Tracy was on such a high that I doubted if anything could upset her for long. Even now, talking to me, she kept sliding her eyes back to where Stewie was talking to one of the chaperons. She couldn't keep her eyes off him for over ten seconds.

Rod went off to get a soda. He'd already downed half a dozen, but he was still thirsty after the game.

Tracy leaned close to me and whispered, "It's all working like a dream, isn't it?"

"I suppose."

"Three cheers for butterflies and for crazy friends who can think up wild and crazy stunts."

"I suppose," I said again.

"You suppose?" Tracy's eyes tightened. She even forgot to check on Stewie for maybe fifteen seconds. "What's the matter with you? This night is your dream come true, and here you are afraid to jump in and enjoy it."

"I don't think that's it. I mean I'm not afraid. And I'm having fun. Rod's a great date."

"I'll say. Of course I wouldn't trade Stewart for him," she said with another quick glance over at Stewie, just to make sure he hadn't vanished or something.

"Of course not."

Her eyes came back to me. "Then what's wrong with you?"

"I think maybe I'm coming down with the flu or something. I've been feeling really rotten all day."

"What's the matter? Do you have butterflies in your stomach?" She laughed at her little joke.

"Cut it out, Tracy. I get enough of that kind of stuff from everybody else without hearing it from my . . ." I hesitated before I finished. "From you." I had been going to say best friend, but I was beginning to wonder if that was true anymore. Best friends were supposed to understand one another without everything being spelled out. She should have known that my date with Rod wasn't exactly as wonderful as I'd expected it to be.

But she only said, "Sorry. Can't you take a joke?" Then her smile disappeared as all at once she was serious again. "Don't look so worried, Wendi. The only thing you're coming down with is love. Quit fighting it, and believe you me, it'll start feeling good instead of rotten."

As I watched her float back to Stewie, I wished I could feel as happy as she was obviously feeling. And Stewie looked just as happy as he put his arm around her waist and guided her back onto the floor just in time for a slow dance.

I turned back to Rod, who was coming toward me, and smiled at him, determined to be a bright, exciting, fun-filled date for the rest of the time I was with him. I could postpone feeling rotten for another half hour or so.

Chapter 9

On the way home, I didn't run out of bright and clever things to say until he turned off on my street. "We're almost there," he said, reaching over for my hand.

"I had a great time, Rod."

He squeezed my hand. "Not yet. The best part is just about to begin."

After that I couldn't think of a word to say while blood pounded through my veins.

As he pulled the car to a stop in front of my house, he said, "It didn't rain, little butterfly girl, but I have the feeling butterflies hide under their little leaves at night, too, don't you?"

"Probably. I'm not the expert on butterflies everybody seems to think."

He put his hand on my cheek. "But you are a frightened little butterfly now. Why? I won't hurt you."

"I guess I'm just sort of new at dating."

"And kissing?"

He leaned over and tipped up my face. Although it was dark in the car, I could see the shape of his face and the shine of his eyes as he studied me for a moment before he dropped his lips down to cover mine.

Closing my eyes, I let him kiss me. I even put one of my hands up around his neck and rubbed my fingers through the hair on the back of his head that I'd grown to know so well in the first weeks of school.

I waited for the bells to go off and the lights to flash, but as he pulled away from me, I only felt relieved that it was over. I hadn't bumped his nose or hiccuped or giggled. I had successfully completed my first kiss.

"That wasn't so bad, was it?" he said.

"Not bad at all." My heart slowed its pounding even though he still had his hand on my cheek. "I guess I'd better go in."

"Already? Surely you want more than one kiss after all these weeks of trying to get me to ask you out."

"I don't know what you're talking about." My heart sank like lead down to my stomach.

"Don't you?" He laughed softly. "Girls are funny. They think boys never know what's going on in their pretty little heads."

"All right. What's going on in mine?"

"Now or at the first of the year?"

I pulled away from him. "What do you mean, at the first of the year?"

"Well, this is what you were hoping for when you pretended not to hear Scary Mary call out your name so you could sit behind me. Allen told me I ought to get you a drooling bib."

"Then it was all just a joke." Tears jumped up in my eyes and spilled over.

"Hey, don't cry. I wouldn't have asked you out for a joke."

"You just said you did." I reached for the door handle. "Well, the joke's gone far enough."

He caught my arm. "Wait, butterfly girl. Don't be so ready to fly away. Maybe it was a little funny at first, but then after I got to know you, it stopped being a joke. You're a nice kid, and I sort of like you."

I sat back and took a deep breath, unable to remember ever feeling so dumb. "I didn't pretend not to hear Mrs. Lunsford call out my name. She didn't."

"Maybe not. Look, I didn't aim to hurt your feelings, but I just can't figure why you're trying to brush me off so quick now when you used to chase after me."

"I didn't figure on ever catching you."

He laughed. "That's the best thing about you, butterfly girl. You're funny. We can have fun together." He stroked my cheek. "I can teach you a thing or two about kissing, and you can teach me all sorts of things about butterflies."

When I didn't say anything he went on. "You do like me, don't you, butterfly girl?"

"Of course I do. You're a great guy."

"Then how about the homecoming dance? I mean Coach Buckley doesn't want us to have steady girls or anything, but he doesn't care if we go to the dance."

Rod Westmore was asking me, Wendi Collins, to the homecoming dance. Rod Westmore. The greatest-looking, most popular guy at Brookfield High. I let the thought circle in my mind for a few minutes, but it didn't bring that flare of accomplishment I'd thought it would a month ago. "Thanks for asking me, but I don't think so," I said.

"Now who's pulling a joke on who?"

"I like you, Rod," I said quickly. "And you were right about me trying to get you to notice me at the first of the year. I might have stood on my head then if it would have done any good. I mean you're a great-looking guy. Better-looking than most of the movie stars."

"Thanks, I guess."

"But I just wouldn't make a good girlfriend for you. I want to be liked for myself, not for who I'm with."

"I like you for yourself."

"That's the nicest thing you've ever said to me," I said, with tears in my eyes again. "And I think if you want to, we can be a great friends, but I don't think we were ever meant to be a couple."

"I can't believe this." Leaning back in his seat, he sounded surprised but not particularly upset. "Let's see. What's the next thing I'm supposed to say? Something like, is there another boy?" His voice deepened dramatically, and I could tell he was smiling. Impulsively I leaned over and brushed his cheek with my lips. "Now she kisses me," he said with a touch of exasperation.

"This way you can keep the coach happy and make him think you're concentrating solely on football. And you won't have to worry about anybody thinking I turned you down. I mean I'm the one who's a joke."

"But you never did tell me if it was another boy."

"Do you remember that night Allen asked me what kind of butterfly I was and I said I was still a caterpillar? Well, maybe I'm just not ready to have boyfriends."

"Your trouble, little butterfly girl, is that you're

124

afraid to try your wings. You're sitting there on the edge of your cocoon wanting to crawl back inside instead of taking off into the unknown.''

"Maybe, but then maybe the sun's just not shining bright enough yet for me to try flying." After looking over at him for a moment, I reached for the door handle. "I did have a great time, Rod."

"Yeah, it was fun. Or at least different." Then before I could push open the door, he caught my arm and said, "Hey, butterfly girl, you won't get mad if I put a butterfly on my bug board, will you? I can't take the chance of getting a bad grade in biology and having the coach come down on me."

"I won't get mad."

The overhead light came on when I opened the door, and I could see his face clearly. As I looked at him, I wondered how in the world I could have ever turned down a chance to go to the homecoming dance with him. But I wasn't sorry.

"You don't care if I don't walk you to the door, do you?" He took a quick look at his watch. "I would, but I'll barely make curfew now and knowing Coach this will be the very night he'll pick to call me. He knew I had a date."

"Sure, go ahead. And thanks again for a great night."

"Anytime, kid. See you Monday."

I hurried up the walk and opened the front door. Rod was already pulling away before I turned to wave.

In the living room, Mom was slumped over on the couch, asleep. "Mom, I'm home," I said.

She opened her eyes slowly, regretfully, as though she didn't want to come away from her dreams. "It's late, Mom. You'd better go to bed."

Mom woke up fully then and looked from me to the clock. "I guess so. It's not but a few hours till we have to leave for the city. You are going with us, aren't you?"

I searched my mind for some reason I was supposed to go with them tomorrow and came up empty. "Why?"

Mom shook her head at me. "Don't you remember? Madelaine's competing tomorrow. I told you about it Thursday in my note. I was hoping you'd take pictures for us."

"Oh." I remembered the note I had tossed into the trash without reading.

"It's just a small competition, but Coach Barton says it'll be a good practice for Madelaine. Of course she won't be able to use her new routine with her new music yet for the floor exercise."

"Then you found some music," I said as I sat down beside her.

"Oh yes, and it's perfect." Her eyes were shining. "I saw her go over the new routine today, and it's going to be wonderful. Coach Barton was ecstatic. Madelaine told him it was all your idea, and he says you must be a genius and he can't wait to meet you."

"Then you found something about butterflies."

"I don't know whether it's about butterflies or not, but it makes you think of butterflies dancing in the sunshine across a field of daisies. It's light and airy and just perfect for Madelaine."

"Because Maddie is light and airy," I said without a pang of jealousy.

"She practically floated above the mat today. Her tumbling runs were as good as I've ever seen her do.

126

Even Coach Barton couldn't find much fault with her tricks, but you'll get to see her tomorrow.''

"Do I have to go?''

"But the pictures you take always turn out so much better than mine.''

"I'll go next time.''

"Are you sure you don't want to go? We'll have to stay overnight, and you wouldn't want to stay here by yourself.''

"I don't know. I've gotten sort of used to it, and I have this project in biology that I've got to get finished by Monday.''

"I suppose you're old enough to stay here alone,'' Mom said slowly. "Maybe you could ask Tracy over.''

"Sure,'' I said. "If she doesn't have a date.''

"All this hasn't been easy on you, has it, Wendi? I mean all this with Madelaine.''

"Or on you.''

"But it's different for me. I'm right out there with Madelaine every time she competes. I'm willing to do anything to see that she has her chance, because her dream somehow is my dream, too.'' Mom looked at me. "But it can't be that way with you, and it shouldn't be. You've got your own dreams.''

I started to say something, but Mom pushed in in front of my words. "Just like now. Here you come home from your first date and all I can do is talk about Madelaine.''

"That's all right, Mom. My dreams aren't anything very special.''

"Everybody's dreams are special. You're special. And I do want to know about your date. That's why I'm not in bed like I ought to be.''

127

"It was okay."

"Just okay?"

"Well, nice then." I thought that was a funny way for me to describe a date with Rod Westmore after dreaming about it for months.

"You look very pretty in your new sweater. I was sure you would when I first saw it in the store. I'll bet all the boys were jealous of Rod."

"I don't know about that, but the girls were jealous of me. I guess Rod's the most chased-after boy in school."

"Did you chase after him?"

"How do you think I got this date?" I laughed a little and turned away from that thought quickly before I had time to think too much about being the joke of Brookfield High. "Do you remember your first date, Mom? Was it as good as you expected?"

She got a funny look on her face and then laughed out loud.

"What's so funny?"

"Arnie Miller," she said. "Well, not really Arnie. I guess I was what was so funny. You see, Arnie was a nice-looking guy with the cutest little mustache. He took me to a movie, and all the time we were there I worried so much about whether his mustache would tickle when he kissed me that I hardly noticed the movie. Then when he brought me home he didn't even kiss me, but Dad asked me what movie we'd seen and I couldn't remember anything about it. By the time Dad would let me go out again, Arnie had shaved his mustache and had another girlfriend."

"I guess it's a good thing Rod and I didn't go to a movie."

"Do you know who won the game?"

"That's an easy one. The Brookfield Tigers won, of course."

As we laughed together, I felt closer to Mom than I had in a long time.

"I guess we'd better go to bed," Mom said, standing up. "Was Jeff at the sock hop?"

"He was there."

"He went with that little Vanessa whatever-her-name-is who's a cheerleader, didn't he? She's a cute little thing."

"I suppose if you like that type." I ran on up to my room before Mom could say any more about Vanessa and Jeff. I'd gotten tired enough of seeing them together all night, and I didn't particularly like thinking about them together now. I mean Vanessa wouldn't be worried about bumping noses or anything else when she kissed a boy. Kissing would come as natural to her as purring to a kitten.

Before I went to sleep I allowed myself one look over at Jeff's window. It was still dark.

When Mom woke me before daylight to make sure I hadn't changed my mind about going with them, I showed her my bugs waiting to be stuck on my board and said, "My grade in biology might not be so hot to begin with. I need to do as good as I can on this project."

"Are you having trouble in biology?" Mom asked with a little frown.

For a few seconds I considered telling her the whole mess, but then she glanced at my clock. Knowing she must be running late, I only said, "Not really. It's just not an easy class."

"I'm not too worried. You always get great grades."

"I might not this time."

Mom smoothed my hair back off my forehead. "We sometimes take you for granted, don't we, sweetheart? You just do everything so well all the time. Your grades, keeping everything going around here while I'm at the city with Madelaine, and then the way you can take such great pictures. Those you took of Madelaine last Sunday turned out super."

I started to protest that I didn't do anything well, but just then there was a loud crash from the bathroom and Maddie yelled for Mom. Mom winced. "I hope it's nothing too serious. You just can't be late to these competitions."

I stayed in bed and listened to them leave. Maddie was chattering like she always does when she's nervous. Maybe nervous wasn't the right word. Frantically excited might describe her better. As she and Mom went down the steps together I could almost see Maddie's feet skimming over the carpet as if she didn't feel the same pull of gravity the rest of us did. Dad's steps down the stairs behind them were heavy and solid. Then they were out the front door, and the car started and slid away toward the city.

"Good luck, little butterfly," I whispered as the quiet of the house settled back around me.

When I woke the second time, sunlight was spreading warm fingers across my bed. Three sunny Saturdays in a row. I could hardly believe it.

I had on my swimsuit and was staring at my dead bugs when Tracy showed up. There weren't very many bugs in the jars. I'd have to take my killing jar out into the sunshine with me.

Frankly I was getting sick of bugs in any shape, form, or fashion, and I couldn't see how it would help me at all to know this three-spotted beetle was from the subfamily Scarabaeidae while this strange-looking four-spotted one with a snout was of the genus *Brentus*. I could write all those yard-long scientific names down, but I never expected to remember them. I had a hard enough time copying them out of the encyclopedia without misspelling them.

When I hollered down to Tracy to come on up, she bounded up the steps and into my room. "I just had to come over to see how everything went last night," she said.

"You could have called."

"My, aren't we the hospitable one this morning?" she said, but nothing could dampen her spirits for long. "Well, tell me all about it."

"There's not much to tell. He brought me home. I told him I had a great time, and he said it was fun. Then I got out and came in the house."

"Did he kiss like a dream?" Tracy sighed.

"Why do you care how Rod kisses? You're the one who said Stewie had expressive lips."

"And he does." Tracy closed her eyes and hugged herself a little.

"I guess you're going with him to the homecoming dance."

"Of course. Stewart and I are going everywhere together." She held out her hand, and there on her finger was a little silver friendship ring.

"It's beautiful."

"It is, isn't it? Stewart said he knew it was a little old-fashioned to give girls rings like this, but he doesn't have a class ring yet and he wanted to give me something to show we were special friends."

"Who'd have ever thought Stewie would be so romantic?"

For a moment Tracy looked ready to jump to his defense, but then she giggled. "Not me. At least not a month ago before all this started with the butterflies and everything. Until I saw him over here and got to know him, I'd never really seen him. You know, he has beautiful eyes, especially when he takes off his glasses."

"I'm glad you had a good time."

She must have heard something in my voice because she came back from cloud nine and said, "Did you and Rod have a fight?"

"Rod and I don't know each other well enough to have a fight."

"Did he ask you to the homecoming dance?"

I sidestepped the truth. "The coach doesn't like for them to have steady girlfriends."

"That doesn't seem to stop Allen and Mary Lou. You'd almost think the two of them were married the way they carry on."

"Allen's not as serious about his football as Rod is. Besides, I just don't think Rod and I are suited for each other. Not as a couple anyway."

Tracy studied my face for a minute. "Did he try something funny last night?"

"Quit trying to make more out of it than there is."

"Well, I told you back when you first got a crush on him that he was stuck-up."

"But you were wrong. Rod's a great guy, but we decided it might be fun to just be friends for a while."

"Friends, eh?" Tracy gave me a funny look, but she only said, "I guess that's better than nothing."

I sort of half nodded, and Tracy seemed to notice

for the first time what I was doing. "Do you have enough bugs?"

"I can't figure out what these two are." I pointed toward a couple of nondescript black bugs. "I'm thinking about labeling them UFI for Unidentified Flying Insect."

"I doubt if Scary Mary would laugh."

"She might," I said. Then I sighed. "It doesn't really matter. She's probably going to slap an F on mine anyway after all the trouble I've caused her."

"She can't do that. You've got most of your bugs."

"Not really, and none of the order Lepidoptera."

"Butterflies?" Tracy asked, but she looked bored. "I'm not even taking biology and I'm getting sick of bugs. Talking about boys is infinitely more interesting." She looked over at me still counting bugs. "And since you don't seem to want to talk about anything interesting, maybe I should just go home."

"Well, if you have to." I didn't even ask her to stay over like Mom had wanted me to.

"Gee, you're great fun today," she said as she turned to leave. I walked down the steps with her. "Oh, by the way, I got your mail when I came in. You got some kind of package."

"Probably something Mom ordered for Maddie."

"No, it's for you. I put it on the front table."

I picked up the small square package. "It's from Jason," I said, recognizing his writing. "But it doesn't feel like it's got anything in it."

"For heaven's sake, open it and see. No telling what it is if it's from Jason."

"He's never sent me anything from school before." I pulled the paper off the box, cut through the tape on the sides with my fingernail, and then lifted

133

off the top. There in a bed of cotton lay a monarch butterfly, a little battered but still an acceptable specimen.

Jason had written a note on the inside of the box top. "Here's a butterfly. It was dead when I found it. Use it. Jason."

I thought of Jason finding the butterfly and taking the trouble to mail it to me, and I had to blink hard to keep back the tears.

"Who'd have ever thought Jason would send you a butterfly? But then I guess it's just like him to give you the solution to your problem."

"How's that?" I looked up at her.

She was still looking at the butterfly. "After all, Wendi, it is already dead. It couldn't hurt to stick a pin in it now."

I looked at the butterfly a long time and reread the note three times before I said, "I don't think I can, Tracy." I pushed the box out toward her. "Why don't you give it to Stewart? That way it won't be wasted."

She looked a little uncomfortable as she said, "The truth is, I'm afraid Stewart hasn't exactly shared our butterfly enthusiasm. He's already got a whole set of lepi-whatever you said."

I felt a curious letdown. "I can't say as I blame him. There's no sense in him messing up his perfect grade point average over a few butterflies."

Tracy looked even more uncomfortable. "Actually I think he was just having fun with Mrs. Lunsford, if you know what I mean."

I stared at her, but she wouldn't meet my eyes. "Are you trying to tell me he was behind the Down with Scary Mary posters? Stewie?" My throat felt tight as I went on. "And you knew about it and didn't tell me?"

When Tracy tried to turn away, I jerked her back around to face me. "I almost got suspended because of those posters," I said.

Tracy finally met my eyes. "I didn't know till last night. I would have told you if I had."

I kept staring at her, not sure I could believe her.

"Honest, Wendi. I knew he was doing something, but I never dreamed he'd put up those Scary Mary posters. I mean Stewie's always been so careful to stay in good with the teachers."

I was so mad I hardly noticed that she'd called him Stewie. I kept thinking about all those posters I had to scrape off the walls and about being called to the office by Mr. Browning and about how the Scary Mary stuff had hurt Mrs. Lunsford whether she would admit it or not.

From what seemed a long way away, I heard Tracy saying, "You've got to believe me, Wendi."

"Why?" I said as some of the red in my mind began to fade.

"Because we're friends."

She looked so genuinely sorry that I had to tell her I believed her, but just because I forgave her didn't mean I had to forgive Stewie. "I'm going to kill him with my bare hands. Or better yet, tell Mrs. Lunsford the truth," I said.

"You can't do that," Tracy said in a panic. "I promised Stewart I wouldn't tell you."

"I don't think I like your 'Stewart' very much."

"I guess I can't blame you, but no real harm was done. You didn't really get suspended or anything."

"No thanks to Stewie."

"He's not perfect." Tracy looked at me pleadingly. "But I like him a lot. Please, Wendi, please don't turn him in. He'd be so mad at me."

"Okay," I said reluctantly. "I suppose what's done is done. But if I see so much as one more poster, I'm going straight to Mr. Browning's office with it and the truth."

"He'll stop. I'll see to it." She glanced up at the clock and said, "I've got to get home. Mom's taking me shopping for something to wear to the dance." She looked back at me and hesitated before she added, "You want to come along?"

"Not today. I've got to label bugs. I'm hoping if I do a super job on the insects I do have Mrs. Lunsford won't flunk me for the whole year."

Tracy looked back down at the butterfly in the box. "Use it, Wendi. Nobody will care."

Chapter 10

After Tracy left I stared at the monarch in its bed of cotton for a long time. Of course Jason expected me to use it in my collection, and what could it hurt?

I softly touched the butterfly's wing before putting the top back on the box and stashing it in the drawer of the little table. I'd decide what to do with it later. Right now the sun was wasting outside.

When I went through the kitchen, I saw the pictures Mom had picked up in the city the day before. The ones of Maddie were as good as Mom had said. Maddie's look of rapt concentration didn't shut out the joy that seemed to radiate from inside her as she practiced her tricks against the background of blue sky and green grass. One picture showed nothing but sky around her as she touched the height of her flip.

A warm feeling of pride soaked through me, but it wasn't just that I was proud of Maddie. I was proud of the picture. I had planned it and caught it perfectly.

When I flipped on through the prints, the butterflies surprised me. I'd almost forgotten taking them with the idea of using them on a Save the Butterflies poster. The monarch resting on a fence post looked ready to take wing at any second while the swallowtail floated on the breeze. I had run ahead of the blue and black butterfly and stopped, waiting for the exact right second to snap the shutter. Then, just to be sure I caught the picture the way I'd wanted to, I'd done it all again.

Just as I'd captured Maddie's special talent in her pictures, I'd captured the special beauty and freedom of the butterflies.

I looked back through the pictures one more time, sorry now I hadn't gone to Maddie's competition after all. My fingers were practically itching to take more pictures.

But I had to get my biology project completed, and I still needed at least ten insects. I stared at my bug-killing jar with distaste before I dropped it in the trash can. I'd killed my last bug.

Then I thought of the F Mrs. Lunsford would be sure to give me if I showed up with only half the required insects. With a sigh, I leaned over to get the jar out of the trash, but as I picked it up, my eyes caught on the picture of the monarch I'd left on top of the stack of photographs.

Setting the jar on the counter, I studied the butterflies. If I could take pictures of butterflies, I could take pictures of other insects as well. I could use all pictures in my insect collection.

I was so excited my hands trembled as I put fresh film in my camera and raced outside. After I'd found and photographed every bug in the yard, I lay back on the lounge chair and shut my eyes, tired but satisfied.

Later I'd take my film to the drugstore that had the fast-developing service. On the way I could surely find enough different insects to finish out my film, but now I was going to concentrate on not thinking about bugs for a few minutes.

I heard a door slam at Jeff's house, but I refused to look over that way. That was another thing I wasn't going to think about. The warm sun poured down, surrounded me, and made me drowsy.

When I woke up, a small yellow sulphur butterfly was perched on my toe while two or three others fluttered around the yard in front of me. Their wings were a deep yellow, and I remembered reading once that perhaps the word butterfly had been coined to describe this very insect, since its color was like butter. I began carefully reaching for my camera without moving my foot.

"He must think your toe is a flower."

I jumped, and the butterfly took to startled flight. When I turned my head, there was Jeff sitting on the ground beside me, looking settled as though he'd been there for some time. "It's not nice to sneak up on somebody when they're asleep," I said crossly.

He grinned. "At least I didn't bring the water hose."

"No. And I'd have killed you if you had."

"You? You wouldn't even hurt a butterfly."

Looking out at the yellow butterflies fluttering between the late-blooming flowers, I counted more than ten now. "Do you really think it would hurt anything if we put them in our insect collections?"

"I don't see how it could. Looks like to me they're having a population explosion." He stood up. "Come on. I'll bet I can catch one first."

I found out quick enough it was true what they said about not being able to catch a butterfly on the wing. It was also true I couldn't catch one of these little fluffs of energy on the wing or not. Each time I was ready to pounce on one that had paused on a flower, he flitted a little to the side and lit on another flower. Jeff wasn't having any more luck than I was.

After he'd chased one all around the yard, he said, "Every time I zig, it zags. We need a net."

"It's hopeless." Out of breath, I sank down in the shade of the garage. "They're absolutely safe from this biology student."

Jeff dropped down beside me. He was in too good shape to be out of breath over that little bit of running, but his face was flushed and I could feel the heat of his body next to mine. For some reason my heart started speeding up even though I was resting now.

Our eyes caught and held as though we'd only just seen one another this very minute, and we were afraid if either of us looked away the other might disappear. Then Jeff put his hand on the back of my neck and pulled my head up close to his. His lips were soft and warm and gentle as they covered mine.

All at once I felt like my bones had melted and I was one of those little yellow butterflies floating along on a gentle breeze in the sunshine. This was the way a kiss should be. Not something you worried about and planned how to do, but something that just happened because the moment was right. And believe me, the moment must have been right.

Then he was lifting his head, and though I wanted the moment to stay like that forever, I had to pick that instant to wonder if he'd kissed Vanessa like that the night before.

"Did you have a good time at the sock hop with Vanessa last night?"

He took his hand away from my head, leaned back

against the garage, and looked up at the sky. "Sure. I had a great time."

His voice was stiff like I'd said something to hurt his feelings, and I felt like crying.

"I could ask you how your date with the one and only great football hero Rod Westmore was."

"You could."

"But I won't." He got up in one quick movement.

I let him walk away while I frantically searched my mind for some way to get him to stay. All I could think of was Jason's butterfly.

"Hey," I called, stopping him before he crossed over into his yard. "Jason sent me a recently deceased monarch if you want it for your insect collection."

"Jason?" He looked back at me with amazement.

"Yeah, Jason. Imagine that. He found out about my 'butterfly nonsense' as he put it when he was home last weekend. So he sent me a butterfly to use."

"Then why don't you use it?"

"I don't know."

"Tell me, Wendi. Would you have put one of the yellow butterflies in your killing jar if we had been quick enough to catch one?"

"No. I may be silly like Jason says, and I'm going to get a bad grade for sure, but I can't kill butterflies."

"Everybody else in the class will use butterflies. All this other stuff with the signs and everything was just fun for them. A way of getting at Mrs. Lunsford."

"I know. And it doesn't matter what they do, but my share of butterflies will stay free as the wind."

"That shouldn't keep you from using the dead one Jason sent you."

"I can't. It just wouldn't be right. Butterflies are too special to me."

"You're pretty special yourself, Wendi," he said before he turned and went on into his house.

I watched his back door for a long time, willing him to come back out and over to my yard again, but it didn't work.

Finally I lay back down on the lounge. As I shut my eyes I could feel Jeff's lips on mine again, and just with the memory my bones melted a little till I felt soft and pliable there in the heat of the sun. I loved him, I thought with a jolt of surprise. And not just as a friend I'd shared teethers and backyard wading pools with, but as someone special and a little mysterious. It seemed strange to think of Jeff as mysterious. A month ago I'd have said I knew him as well as I knew the back of my own hand, but while I hadn't been looking, he'd changed. We'd both changed.

In my mind I listed the surprises I'd had this week. Rod turning out not to be the boy of my dreams after all but someone I'd like to be friends with. Maddie telling Coach Barton about me, her ordinary sister, and him wanting to meet me. Mom saying she was proud of me. Jason sending me the butterfly. The pictures. And the biggest surprise of all, Jeff kissing me.

Unable to stand sitting still a minute longer, I grabbed my camera from under the lounge. If I couldn't catch one of the yellow butterflies with my hands, I could with the lens. After I tracked the butterfly, waiting for the right moment to snap the shut-

142

ter, I went inside to get dressed. I had a lot to do, and the first thing was to get my film developed.

The next day I didn't see Jeff except in his car leaving with his family for the country to visit his grandparents. His mom called and asked if I wanted to go along, but I made my excuses. I needed time to get used to this new way I felt about Jeff.

I spent the afternoon mounting my photographs and writing out the insect classifications under them, and by the time Maddie came in flushed with victory I had my insect collection ready to turn in the next morning. I wasn't sure Mrs. Lunsford would accept my collection, but as I looked over the photographs I was proud of my work.

Seeing the pictures of the monarch made me remember the butterfly Jason had sent me. I took it out of the box and fixed it so it was ready to mount. There was no reason not to take it to school and let someone else use it.

Monday morning it looked like half the people who came to school were carrying Styrofoam boards full of dead bugs. Not wanting to see the butterflies, I avoided looking at them. When I started down the hall to Mrs. Lunsford's room to turn in my collection, which I had covered up so nobody could see the pictures, Rod was in front of me.

"Wait up, Rod," I called. I was glad when he stopped and smiled because then I knew for sure he wasn't mad about Friday night.

"Well, if it isn't the butterfly girl."

"Did you get all your insects?" I asked.

He made a face. "I lack a couple. There's only so many bugs in the world, and half of them wouldn't let me catch them. Now if they'd been footballs . . ."

"I've got one you can have if you need it." I pulled out the box with the monarch in it.

"Why, butterfly girl, I didn't think you would do such a thing." He looked at me with real surprise.

"My brother found it for me after it was already dead. You can have it if you want it."

"You're not going to use it?" When I shook my head he shrugged and said, "Sure, why not? I need all the help I can get in biology."

I gave him a blank label, and he wrote out the information and then pinned it on his board with the butterfly. "They are pretty," he said as he looked at it. "But once they're dead, they're dead. Right, kid?"

"I guess so."

"Hey, kid, would you mind taking this on into Scary Mary's room for me? I need to see the coach a minute before the bell rings."

"Okay." I took his board. "See you later."

I met Jeff coming down the hall away from the biology room. He looked at the two boards I was carrying and said, "You did two?"

"One of them is Rod's."

"Oh." The word was quiet and tight like his eyes. "I see you gave him the butterfly."

"I offered it to you first."

"So you did." He looked up at the clock in the hall and not at my face. "You'd better hurry. The bell's about to ring."

With a heavy heart, I watched him rush off up the hall. My heart didn't get any lighter as I took the boards on into the biology room and laid them on the table with the others already there. The bright colors of butterflies and moths dotted the boards.

Several of Mrs. Lunsford's homeroom students

were already in their seats, but the room was silent as always. Mrs. Lunsford looked up from her desk and said, "Good morning, Miss Collins."

Meeting her eyes, I answered, "Good morning, Mrs. Lunsford."

"This is the day, isn't it?"

"Yes, ma'am." A couple of other kids had brought in their insect collections and were casting furtive glances our way, but they were afraid to linger.

"I hope you made the right decision," she said.

"I think I did. Now if I can be excused, I wouldn't want to be late for homeroom."

"Very well." She peered past me toward the spread of insect collections, but she didn't move from her chair.

By the time I walked into biology late that day and found my seat, I was reconciled to receiving a bad grade. While I might have made the right decision for me, it wouldn't be the one Mrs. Lunsford thought was right.

Mrs. Lunsford started out the class by saying, "Though I've only had a chance to grade a few of your insect collections, I want to compliment most of you on your fine effort to include all the orders of insects I specified." She paused a moment before she went on. "Now we'll see how much you've learned."

The rest of the hour was spent taking a pop quiz on the different orders of insects and their body parts. I breezed through it because I had memorized it just in case she decided to spring a test on us. After all I'd have to make perfect grades the rest of the year to offset the bad grade she was sure to give me for my bug collection.

When the bell rang, the words I'd been expecting came. "Miss Collins, stay after class."

I waited till everybody else had gone out of the room before I approached her desk.

"This is getting to be a regular habit, isn't it, Miss Collins? I trust this will be the last time." She looked at me with raised eyebrows and a smile in her eyes.

"Yes, ma'am. I think my rebellion has come to an end."

"Ah, but you never did bend to the rules, did you? I want to know something. Was it just the fear of losing face with the other students?"

"No, ma'am," I answered carefully. "This Save the Butterflies campaign probably seemed silly to you, but I really believe butterflies are worth saving."

"But we've already established they're not in danger of extinction."

"Yes, ma'am. But I guess I wanted to do more than just protect them. I wanted everybody else to see butterflies like I do."

"And how's that?"

"I don't know if I can explain it. To me, butterflies are like a special gift nature has given us," I said. "When I was little I used to chase after them and wish I could be one just for a few minutes, and even now when I see one skipping through the air or gliding softly on the wind it makes me smile inside. I just couldn't kill them for a school project."

She leaned back in her chair and studied me for a moment. "I think you mean all that, but of course you must realize many butterflies and moths are pests, the same as houseflies and mosquitoes. And they're not all beautiful."

"They're all beautiful in their own way."

She really smiled, this time all the way to her lips. "But then all of nature is, don't you agree? There's the miracle of the bumblebee in flight and the uniqueness of yellow-striped wasps and velvet red ants, all beautiful in their own way," she said with feeling. "Just as every child is unique and beautiful in some special way."

Her words shot home to my heart and surprised me. Everything was surprising me the last few days, as if I'd been walking around with my eyes shut and only now had I dared to really open them and look around. "You really like kids, don't you?"

"Of course I do," she said and then changed the subject abruptly. "Your photographs are not quite what I asked for, but the insects show up in them quite well."

I held my breath as I waited for her to go on. After a moment, she said, "I've decided to give you a C minus on your collection. Your information on the insects is impeccably correct, or I would have given you a lower grade. Also, had the rest of the class pretended to share your convictions in order to avoid doing the assignment, I might have had to make more of an example of you."

"Yes, ma'am." A weight fell off my shoulders as I felt more like I'd just gotten an A plus than a C minus.

"Only one other student failed to include a specimen of the order Lepidoptera. I've given him a straight C. You'll both have to work hard to pull your grades back up to the high levels you've maintained before now."

"Yes, ma'am." I wanted to ask who the other student was but thought better of it.

"That will be all, Miss Collins," she said in dismissal.

I took two steps toward the door before impulsively turning back to her desk. "I'm sorry if I caused you a hard time. I didn't expect the other kids to take up on it and turn it on you the way they did. They didn't really care about butterflies. They were just trying to upset you."

She looked up at me as though surprised I'd dared to keep talking after I'd been dismissed. After a minute, she said, "I've had a number of students who've tried to cause me a hard time, as you say. I've never had trouble handling any of them. Of course you're a little different from most troublemakers," she added with a smile.

I wanted to smile back, but I wasn't sure I should.

She said, "You know I think I might just miss these little talks we've had. Maybe we can get together sometime and compare notes on the beauty of nature, Miss Collins."

"I'd like that." This time my smile just slipped out.

"By the way, your photographs showed imagination and talent. Of course your butterflies are lovely and seem ready to fly out of the pictures, but I like your stag beetle that seemed to be ready to attack. And your nest teeming with paper wasps. You didn't get stung, did you?"

"Only once," I said. "But you really thought my pictures were good?"

"Very good. You have a special gift, Wendi. One not many people have. You can see pictures."

"Thank you." I was trembling inside again, not

from fear now but from pleasure because of her praise. "I love to take pictures."

"I can tell. You should keep working at it, and if you ever have any more nature shots, why don't you bring them by? I've always been interested in nature photography. I might even be able to give you some pointers about tracking down your subjects."

"Yes, ma'am, that sounds like fun."

As I went out of the room, I thought that Mrs. Lunsford might turn out to be the best teacher I'd ever have.

Jeff was waiting for me in the hall. "You're actually smiling," he said. "Here I was, ready to charge in to your rescue at the first scream, and you come out smiling."

"I like her."

He looked at me as though he knew for sure this time I had completely lost my mind.

"And you were wrong about her not liking anything but bugs and snakes. She likes kids and photography."

"Now I know you've been spending too much time alone with your bugs."

I laughed. "Of course she did give me a C minus, but that sounded pretty good when I was expecting an F."

"Then I guess I got a C minus, too. There goes the old GPA."

"So you were the other one who was influenced by my rebellion," I said, wanting to hug him. "Actually you only got a C. I think she expects us to make it up with a lot of hard work." I looked over at him a little shyly. "Maybe we can study together."

"I thought you already had a study partner," he said while his eyes tightened.

"You mean Rod?"

"Who else?"

"It's funny about Rod," I said as we began walking up the hall. "I used to think he was the most gorgeous and unapproachable guy in the world. Maybe being unapproachable made him that much more gorgeous, but now that I know him, we're just friends."

"You mean he didn't ask you to the homecoming dance?"

I started to shake my head, but I had never lied intentionally to Jeff in all the years I'd known him. "Well, actually he did, but you've got to promise not to tell anybody."

"Why? Everybody will see you there with him."

"I told him I couldn't go with him. We just aren't a couple, if you know what I mean."

The tightness went out of Jeff's eyes, and light fairly exploded from them. "I know what you mean."

"Of course, I suppose you're going with Vanessa. After all, like you said, no boy in his right mind would ever turn down a Vanessa."

"She's not my type," Jeff said with a smile.

"What is your type?" Hope sprang up inside me like a butterfly taking wing.

"I told you that once before. Remember?"

"Oh, yeah. Let's see. She had to be shorter than you and something about being witty and intelligent and pretty with good bones like Mrs. Lunsford's, wasn't it?"

"Something like that."

"I'm shorter than you." I looked up at him out of the corner of my eyes.

"That's true." He didn't look at me as we went out of the school into the sunshine.

"I used to make good grades before today. So maybe that means I'm sort of intelligent."

"True," he agreed again. He turned toward the parking lot, and I followed him.

"I don't know about witty, but I've been told I have good bones."

"Egads!" He turned on me suddenly, grabbed my arms, and held me away from him. "It is you," he said in his deepest voice. "All these years of living right next door to you, and I never saw you till now. My dream girl!"

"Stop it, Jeff. Everybody will think you're crazy."

"I am." He took hold of my hand. "Crazy about you. I have been for months, but you refused to notice till now." He looked over at me and said, "You wouldn't happen to be free to go out to the cross-country meet with me, would you?"

"I'm free as a butterfly. Are you going to win your race?"

"There's every chance of it."

"Good, I can take pictures of you as you cross the finish line. I take great pictures, you know."

"I know, but I was thinking more about a victory kiss."

I blushed. "I'm not too good at victory kisses. That's more Vanessa's style."

"Vanessa? Vanessa who?"

I laughed and punched his shoulder while my pulse sped up at the thought of kissing him again.

Later, as I waited for Jeff to finish the race, different little butterflies kept dancing past me in the air. Here and there they would light to rest while they spread their wings to bask in the sun's warmth. That warmth would supply them with the energy to fly again.

The sun was shining brightly now, warming me through and through. I felt just like one of the butterflies as I soaked up the sunshine. I'd stepped out of the shadows of Jason's brilliance and Maddie's gymnastic talent and found a special talent of my own. I could see pictures.

When I thought about it, I knew Jason and Maddie had never intended to cast me in a shadow, and maybe they really hadn't. Perhaps I had made my own shadows and gathered them around me on purpose so that I'd have an excuse for my shortcomings. But now I was opening my wings and ready to fly off in search of violets in the snow. One thing for sure, when I found those violets, I'd get a great picture.

After making sure I had plenty of film for Jeff's finish line picture, I raised my camera to my eye and began framing and snapping pictures.